A CHRISTMAS
WISH

A CHRISTMAS WISH

JOSEPH PITTMAN

KENSINGTON PUBLISHING CORP.
http://www.kensingtonbooks.com

KENSINGTON BOOKS are published by

Kensington Publishing Corp.
119 West 40th Street
New York, NY 10018

ISBN-13: 978-0-7582-6672-9
ISBN-10: 0-7582-6672-3

First Kensington Trade Paperback Printing: October 2011
First Kensington Mass Market Printing: October 2012

10 9 8 7 6 5 4 3 2

Printed in the United States of America

This one's for . . .

Pittman Family Christmas

Acknowledgments

Many thanks to everyone at Kensington for embracing the world of Linden Corners, with particular appreciation to the wonderful Audrey LaFehr.

Let it be said that of all who give gifts,
these two were the wisest.

—O. Henry, "The Gift of the Magi"

AUTHOR'S NOTE

You've been here before, this place called Linden Corners. There was once the tale of a man, a woman, a young girl, a windmill . . . and a terrible storm that forever changed their lives. Many readers wondered what happened next. This story tells the next chapter. If you are new to the inspiring, enduring tale of the windmill, you need no prior knowledge, as this story stands alone.

You are cordially invited to celebrate the holidays with Brian, Janey, and the rest of the Linden Corners family. Turn the page; there are special gifts waiting to be unwrapped. . . .

PROLOGUE

*Theirs was a seemingly unbreakable bond, one that
had been built by the power of the wind and by the
presence of the mighty windmill. Today the windmill
spun its special brand of magic, even as the harsh
cold of winter approached and nature readied to hi-
bernate for the long, dark months ahead. On this
Wednesday afternoon in November, he found himself
walking through the light coating of snow that covered the ground, venturing beneath the turning sails.
It was here, on this eve of the holiday season, he
sought inspiration and knowledge and strength, all of
which he would need to navigate his way through the
memories of a past tinged with sadness, one that
threatened to undo their fragile happiness. Because as
wonderful as they were together, the days and especially the nights hadn't always been easy, and the coming holiday season would prove to be the most trying
time yet, a test of that bond.*

"Annie, sweet Annie, can you hear me?" he asked,

his voice a hint above a whisper. He hoped the swirling wind would carry his words forward, upward. "I need your help, Annie. Janey needs your help, and I know you're the only one who can show me—who can show us—the way through this difficult time. Thanksgiving is just around the corner, Annie, and how I wish you were here to celebrate with us. It would have been our first—yours and mine, with Janey. The three of us together, trimmings complementing the bounty of our love. But that's not how things worked out. We are two only, and we both miss you. Before long, Christmas will be upon us, and if we can get through a holiday based on joy, on celebration, I think we'll be fine, just fine. Until then, Annie, I just can't predict how Janey will react to certain situations. Can you help me, can you show me the way to make this holiday a special one for your precious daughter? She's only eight and she's alone, except for me, and sometimes I wonder, Annie, am I enough for her?"

There was no answer, not today. Snowflakes fell lightly all around him, the wind was gentle and the sails of the windmill spun slowly. It was as though the old mill could reach out with those giant arms and embrace the quiet soon to descend on the tiny village of Linden Corners, on its residents and on its treasured way of life. On a Christmas wrapped in tragedy, somehow able to transport them beyond their grief.

For this man, a kind but broken man named Brian Duncan, this coming season would be a new experience, knowing the success of the holidays rested solely on his weighted shoulders. And as much as he looked forward to celebrations, of joys, of shopping and of gift giving, there were times when his warm heart was frozen with fear. Uncertainty could stop him in his step at a moment's notice, now being one of those moments.

As they prepared to journey beyond the comfort of Linden Corners—he and Janey taking their first official trip out of town—panic once again seized him, a feeling he usually sensed only after Janey had gone to sleep. A time when the night awakened his insecurities. Often he went to where he could feel Annie's presence the most, seeking her wisdom. Standing now in the shadow of the windmill—of Annie's windmill—he began to realize she couldn't always be there for him. Some decisions he had to make on his own.

"I told my mother, Annie, that I wasn't coming for Thanksgiving unless she made peach pie," Brian said with a touch of levity he thought was needed. He had been introduced to the sweet, gooey pastry just this past summer on a picnic high above the lazy Hudson River, on a rocky bluff he had subsequently named for her. "Mother claimed never to have heard of such a thing. I had to search your recipe box, and even after I found it I doubted it would taste the same. Sweet it would be, but missing that special ingredient you sprinkled into the mix—love. A piece of that pie for Janey was crucial, knowing it's a piece of you. To make her feel at home even when she's not."

There were more questions, more requests. Brian spoke and he listened. And still there was no answer, just gentle, flowing wind and falling snowflakes and the languid spin of the sails. Nothing was different, no sign came to him that he'd been heard. Just then Brian smiled, perhaps interpreting this calm silence as an acknowledgment that if the wind didn't see fit to shift its direction, neither should he. Steady the course, follow your instinct. Trust your heart.

"Okay, Annie, I think I hear you now," he said with a wry smile.

She was like that, mysterious, elusive, even when she'd been in his arms.

He removed his glove and placed a bare hand on the windmill's wooden door, as though searching for a pulse from inside. Its touch was cold. Then, turning back toward the farmhouse, he saw young Janey emerging from over the hill, her fingers laced through those of Gerta Connors, neighbor and friend, honorary grandmother. They both waved at him, with Janey suddenly breaking free of her hold. Janey began to run down the hill, her boots making faint impressions on the snow, as though she was barely touching the ground.

"Brian, Brian, I'm ready for our trip, come on, let's go. We've got a long drive ahead of us," she said with easy glee, conjured from her redoubtable spirit. Where a small girl stored such energy, Brian didn't know. Then she wrapped herself around his waist and held him tight.

"I was just making sure everything was secure," he said. "I see now that it is."

Together, they made their way back up the hill where Gerta waited patiently. Gerta, who had invited them to spend Thanksgiving with her and her four grown daughters, Gerta, who had herself faced terrible loss this past year and persevered, just like them all. It was a Linden Corners trait. Brian had politely declined her invitation. Maybe they both needed this first holiday with their own families, he explained. Holidays were about families, she should be with hers and he, his.

"My mother, she needs her family during these times more so than any other time of year," Brian stated with *little explanation. He didn't often speak of his family; they hadn't shared his recent journey, didn't understand his new life.* "It's a time of year when the Duncan family remembers what we have and what we lost. Maybe the only time we do remember. We so rarely understand each other."

In every family there were both treasures lost and found, Gerta had said with her customary grace and understanding.

Back at the farmhouse, Brian Duncan and Janey Sullivan said their good-byes to Gerta with quiet hugs and heartfelt emotions, and then piled into Brian's car. Suitcases were already stored in the trunk, ready to travel. Was he? Brian wondered.

"Ready?" *Brian asked Janey. Just to be sure.*

"I already said so," *she replied, not without a sense of exasperation that reminded him of the young girl he'd met at the start of summer, before anything had happened. Of the time they had first met that sweet summer day, right here, at the base of the windmill.* "Why, did you change your mind?"

Brian realized she was giving him a chance to change his mind. He grinned at her maturity, her intuitiveness. Sometimes he wondered which of them was the adult, which the child.

"The open road awaits us," *he said.*

Soon they were tucked in their seats and then they had pulled out of the driveway, tires crunching on the small amount of snow in the driveway. Then the winding road captured them, taking them out of Linden Corners, passing the windmill one last time as the car rounded a curve. Janey waved to it, while Brian, smiling nonetheless, kept his eyes on the road. Because he'd already made his wish upon the wind, and it was up to nature now to send his message to that special place where all his wishes belonged.

Christmas was coming.

Surprises awaited them all, not all of them to be unwrapped.

A season of love, of hope, was just around the corner.

They would be back in Linden Corners to celebrate.

For now, it was time to learn about each other, of what lived inside their hearts.

PART 1

OLD
TRADITIONS

CHAPTER 1

If tradition dictates the direction of your life, then it was inevitable that my mother called me two weeks before Thanksgiving to ask whether I would be joining the family for our annual dinner. Every year she makes the same call, every year she asks in her deliberately unassuming way, and every year I respond in my expected fashion. Yes, of course, where else would I be? This year, though, so much had changed—in my life and in my parents' lives, too—that I had to wonder whether the notion of tradition belonged to a bygone era, appreciated only by thoughts of the past, no longer put into practice. How I answered my mother on this day proved that indeed change was in the air, a first step toward tomorrow. Because I informed her that before I could give her an answer, I needed to consult first with Janey.

"Brian, dear, that's very sweet, but you don't

ask children what they want to do. You tell them," she stated matter-of-factly.

"No, Mother, Janey and I, we're a team. We make decisions together."

"Brian, dear, you have so much to learn about children."

Actually, I thought my mother had a lot to learn about her son.

I had been in the kitchen at the farmhouse, mulling over dinner. I hung up and was left to brood the remainder of the day while I cooked, even when Janey came home from school filled with an undimmed light that usually brightened me. I put on my best front as she busily talked about her day. We ate a bland chicken, turkey's everyday fill-in, and still I didn't bring up the idea of the holiday. I waited until bedtime to ask Janey her thoughts on the subject of the coming holiday.

"Thanksgiving? Away from Linden Corners?"

I nodded. "It's your call."

"Do you want to go, Brian?"

"I will if you will," I replied.

"That sounds evasive."

"Where did you learn such a big word like that?"

She rolled her eyes. Vocabulary had never been an issue with Janey. "See, evasive."

I laughed. "Okay, okay. Yes, I'd like to go."

"Good. Then I will if you will," she said, her smile uplifting. "Funny, I get to meet your family. I never thought about them before. That you have parents . . . do you have a big family? Where are they? Do they have a dog. . . ."

"Slow down, slow down. All in good time."

"I'm just curious. Up until now you've always been . . . well, you've been Brian."

"We all come from somewhere."

She thought about that a moment, and I feared it would lead the conversation down a path she wasn't ready for. I certainly wasn't ready for it. But then she just innocently stated, "I can't wait."

Her sudden pause had me wondering what else she was thinking. You could always see the wheels of her mind turning, almost as though they spun her eyeballs.

"Is your mom like mine?"

No, my mind said. I chose not to answer that one directly. "Everyone is their own person."

"Evasive," she said.

I couldn't help it, I laughed. "So, it's agreed, we go. You and me, hand in hand."

"Hand in hand," Janey agreed.

That's how it worked with us.

As night fell and Janey slept, I phoned my mother back and told her to add two plates to the Duncan family's dinner table, that the Linden Corners faction of the family would join them.

"You know how much this means to me, Brian."

Yes, I did.

And while accepting the invitation may have been a relatively smooth process at the time, now, as we turned the corner off Walnut Street in Philadelphia and were only two blocks from my parents' stately new home, anxiety and trepidation ran through me like a monsoon. Sweat beaded on my brow, nerves taking control once I'd parked. The trip had taken us six hours (with a dinner break), but really, it had been an even longer time coming. Nine months had passed since I'd last seen my parents, and during that elapsed time my world had drastically changed in a way none of us could have predicted, myself at the top of that list. I had quit my well-paying job as a thankless corporate drone, sublet my tiny New York apartment, and left behind the supposed woman of my dreams. Setting out on a journey of self-discovery, I had landed in a place that was not far from all I'd known in terms of miles, yet worlds away. I'd met Annie Sullivan and I'd loved her and then I'd lost her, we all had, and as a result I had been given the care of her only daughter, eight-year-old Janey Sullivan, a wonder of a girl, the true one of my dreams. Since then, I'd been very proprietary in terms of exposing Janey to new things. I hadn't allowed any visitors, not friends or family from beyond Linden Corners, wanting this time of transition between me and Janey to take shape without any further disruption. Even now I had my concerns about taking this precious girl out from the safe confines of her life, but realized, too, there was a time for everything, even for moving forward.

"Which house is it?" Janey asked, pointing out the car window at the long row of houses lining both sides of the dimly lit street. This was Society Hill, where both Federal- and Colonial-style town houses prevailed, these classic, restored structures adorning each side of the tree-lined street. It was a sea of brick and white lattices. I didn't blame Janey for being confused; all the houses looked the same. Still, I indicated the building on the far left corner. "With the porch light on."

"Good thing they have that light, since it's so dark. How else would we find it?"

"Well, Janey, I do have the address."

"Oh," she replied with a giggle that made me grin, a good thing right now. Settled my nerves to see how relaxed Janey was.

We had parked on a side street, left the suitcases behind for now. We had enough baggage with us already. So, with Janey's hand in mine, our unlikely team made our way toward the upscale residence of Kevin and Didi Duncan. For years they had lived in the Philly suburbs (in the house I'd grown up in) and then had just this past summer done the opposite of all their friends. They had gone urban, selling the old house and instead buying this very nice home in this very nice section of the City of Brotherly Love. Some investments of Dad's must have really paid off. I had yet to see it myself, thinking this was a good thing, there were no memories of past holidays awaiting me behind those doors. Neutral territory. Though you can never really escape your memories, no matter the walls you've built up, your mind can tear them down when it wants, prompted sometimes by the simplest of senses. As we reached the steps, I looked down at Janey's freckled face and asked, "Ready?"

"You keep asking that," she said. "I think the question is, are you ready?"

"And I think the answer is: Not really."

"Silly—they're your parents, Brian."

As if Janey's words were a magic key, the front door opened and a bath of light from inside illuminated us, sending our shadows retreating to the sidewalk. Yet we stepped forward to where my mother waited in the entranceway. She was dressed in a simple navy skirt and white blouse, a string of pearls dangling from her neck. Perfume wafted in the breeze. Her familiar scent. See what I mean about memories? I had the picture of my mother from years ago, tucking me into bed before she and my father went out to dinner. She smelled the same then, now. What had changed was her hair—she'd allowed it to go gray, and it was salon perfect. She wouldn't be Didi Duncan if not properly attired, even at this hour.

"Well, who have we here?" she asked.

"Your son," I replied, and then Janey said, "And me, I'm Janey."

My mother moved off the top step and gave me an embrace that felt more like an air-kiss before bending down so her face was level with Janey's. "Well, you're a pretty thing, aren't you, Jane?"

"Janey," I corrected her.

She ignored me, keeping her focus on Janey. "That's such a childish name, now, don't you think?"

"I am a child," Janey remarked.

"Nonsense, dear. You've grown tremendously the last few months, haven't you? Come in, come in, the both of you."

And we did, shutting out the encroaching cold behind us. We entered a hallway crafted lovingly with antique wood, and then were ushered down to the living room, where a warm fire was blazing in the large fireplace. My father, Kevin Duncan, sat beside the crackling fire in a wingback leather chair, still dressed in his business suit, the tie still on, the top button to his shirt still clasped. That was the thing about my father. *Still* was a word that described him perfectly. He never changed. He was reading the *Wall Street Journal* and on the table near him was a tumbler filled with his traditional dry Manhattan, the successful entrepreneur in relaxation mode. When he saw us enter, he gently set the paper down on a nearby matching ottoman.

"Hello, son, it's good to see you," he said, shaking my hand with his strong, firm grip. His greeting was as efficient and businesslike as ever; it was just his way, all he knew. He was a tall man, six four and built strongly, and I imagined in his office, even if he hadn't been the boss he would still strike an intimidating pose. Yet a surprising feat happened on this evening. As Janey poked out from behind me, she craned her neck up high so she could see my father and that's when she exclaimed with wide eyes, "Wow, you're big." The stern businessman's face crumpled and a smile found its way to his ruddy face.

"What ho! Well, let's get a look at you, young lady," he said.

"You'd have to sit on the floor to do that."

Kevin Duncan was a big, barrel-chested man, with thick gray hair and a pair of glasses upon his nose, and right now the figure of the man who had always intimidated me actually laughed— something he wasn't exactly known for. Then, instead of bending down as Janey suggested, he lifted the little girl into those big arms of his and I realized that the impossible had been accomplished, Janey had softened the heart of a moneyed giant. I felt pent-up tension leave my shoulders and I realized then that maybe this Thanksgiving wouldn't be so bad. My mother had followed behind us, witnessed the entire exchange between her husband and her . . . my goodness, I almost thought *granddaughter.* I would have to watch my words; Janey and I to this point had avoided all such labels, all such complications.

The four of us settled into the living room and talked genially, Janey enjoying a glass of apple juice and me a seltzer with ice, while my father and mother drank their Manhattans. Their attention remained focused mostly on Janey. They asked her questions about school and friends, nothing about her mother, Annie, or the difficult times this girl had already known in her life. There was no mention of the windmill that had brought us together. As they chatted, I sat on the edge of my seat, waiting anxiously for any misstep.

About ten o'clock, the excitement of the long trip and of Janey meeting my parents finally taking its toll, it was decided we had best get Janey to bed. I retrieved the suitcases from the car and attempted to get Janey settled into her room. She'd gotten her second wind apparently, so busy was she looking at the old photographs my parents had hung on the walls.

"Is that you, Brian?" Janey asked, pointing to a geeky teen posing for his high school graduation picture. I was seventeen. I looked twelve. When I told her it was, she laughed. "You look different now—better." As I thanked her, she pointed to the other two similarly styled portraits that hung above mine, one of a dark-haired, handsome young man, the other a young woman with eyes that dominated the frame. Again, high school graduation pictures. "Who are they?" she asked.

"Well, one is Rebecca; she's my sister."

"She's pretty. And who's the other guy? He doesn't look so . . ."

"Geeky? Like me?"

"Yeah," she said, with an impish smile.

Before answering her question, I stared at the photograph that was up for discussion, thought of the memories his rugged good looks inspired. For a second I looked around for the trophies and awards, the ribbons and framed citations that adorned his walls, and then remembered this was no longer his room. Not even the house he'd grown up in, any of us, actually. Suddenly I was surprised that the photos had been placed on the walls here, not packed away like other memories. I wondered how my parents had felt packing up the old house, saying good-bye to a room that had remained fixed in time. Then I answered.

"That's my brother, Philip."

Our conversation was quickly interrupted as

my mother came brushing through the doorway. She cleared her throat knowingly. Photographs were not something she wished to discuss. When she saw what little progress I'd made in getting Janey to sleep, she summarily tossed me out.

"Honestly, what do you know about caring for little girls, Brian?"

My mother liked to ask questions, but she seldom waited for answers. Tonight was one of those occasions, despite the fact I could have answered her with easy confidence. Because I knew a lot. Janey had helped me in figuring out the curious mind of a growing child, oh she had helped me plenty. But I let my mother enjoy her fussing over Janey, said my good nights, receiving back a huge hug from Janey and a polite smile from my mother, and finally retreated to the other guest room. And as I fought to find sleep that night, I hoped that tomorrow and in the coming weeks I would be able to reciprocate the feelings behind Janey's warm hug. She was in a strange house, meeting strange people, and even though they were my relatives, being here couldn't have been the easiest thing. And it was only the beginning of the holiday season. How much she would need me nearly scared me. How much I would need her terrified me.

CHAPTER 2

We would be eight people for a four o'clock dinner, my mother informed us when we woke, and I didn't relish the idea of just hanging around the house all day, watching her cook and my father read. Eight-year-old girls need far more stimulation. So did I. We were also asked by my mother in her not-so-unsubtle way to "not be underfoot." Bundling up for the unseasonably cold November day, Janey and I escaped the house and spent a good portion of the morning touring the nearby historic district of Philadelphia, including the Liberty Bell and Constitution Hall, though most of the sites were understandably closed down for the holiday. Still, it gave us an opportunity to escape while preparations were made.

"Who's coming to dinner?" Janey asked me at one point.

It was a good question. I hadn't asked and my mother hadn't offered.

"Guess we'll have to wait and find out."

Janey gave me a querulous look. Wondering, no doubt, why I didn't want to know.

We returned at just after two to see the table had been set with my grandmother's fine china and flatware, crystal water tumblers and wineglasses, too, another Duncan family tradition. As kids, we were warned, "You break it . . . you'll regret it." My mother meant it. Even back then she was not known for her warm and fuzzy moments. Also, we realized upon our return that we were not alone, the party of four had now expanded to six. The first guests had arrived, my parents' best friends and my father's business partner, Harry Henderson, and his (third) wife, Katrina, both of whom sat in the living room with glasses of wine and nibbling on cheese and crackers, both of them impeccably dressed. Both Janey and I changed into more suitable clothes for my mother's formal Thanksgiving, returning downstairs for proper introductions. I had met the Hendersons on numerous occasions, so this time it was Janey in the spotlight, and as she politely smiled at them, I wondered how much they'd been briefed on Janey's situation—and found out sooner than I had wanted.

"Why, you're very pretty," Harry said.

"Yes, it's very nice to meet you, Janey," Katrina Henderson said. "I bet Brian's just the best dad. You're very lucky."

A silence descended on the room, the crackling of the fire the only audible sound. My father looked at me with apology in his eyes and my mother put a hand to her mouth, trying in vain to keep the sharp "eek" from coming out. It was Janey, though, who took simple control of the awkward situation when she simply, innocently, and without judgment, said, "Oh, Brian's not my dad. He's . . . he's Brian, and he takes very good care of me."

"Of course he does, dear," my mother said, coming up behind Janey, nearly forcing her from the room with the promise of a sweet treat waiting for her in the kitchen. As though such an obvious action could remove the uncomfortable silence that settled over the room. I stared after Janey, wondering if I should go after her. Finally someone found their voice and I remained.

"I'm so sorry, Brian, I didn't know how to refer to you," Katrina said, "and, well, you must admit, it's a disagreeable situation to be placed in."

"If you think so, imagine how Janey feels. Excuse me," I said, glad to escape their company. I went to check on Janey.

I found her sitting at the kitchen table, drinking a glass of soda while my mother basted the turkey; and here I thought she was comforting Janey. I asked my mother if I could have a moment alone with Janey, and thankfully the ringing of the doorbell saved me from having to ask twice. Guess our other guests had arrived. Gee, I could hardly wait to see who else my mother had lured into her Thanksgiving trap. She tossed down a dish towel and asked that I attend the turkey; "it needs attention."

Well, so did Janey. "You okay?" I asked.

She nodded while taking a prolonged sip from the glass.

"You say the word, we can go home, probably be home in time to . . ."

"To sleep," she said with exasperation. "It's a long drive, remember?"

"We'll leave first thing tomorrow morning, okay?"

"You promise?"

"Cross my heart," I said, and made the motion to mirror my promise.

She set the glass down, scrunching her nose at me. "Brian, what's a tradition?"

"It's . . . well, it's when you do the same thing all the time," I said, knowing that wasn't the best definition I could come up with. "Okay, here's an example. You know how I explained that I have always had Thanksgiving dinner with my parents? That's a tradition. And at Christmastime, we always decorate the tree the night before the big day, just in time for Santa to come and deliver all those great presents. It's the way we've done it year after year, from even before my parents had any children. I think that's how it worked when they were kids, too. How their parents celebrated."

"Wow, Christmas Eve? That's really late for putting up the tree. Mom and I, we always chop down our own tree over at Green's Farms and then set it up long before Christmas, like two weeks ahead."

"See, that's a tradition, Janey. It's your tradition."

"Oh," she said, which made her smile, knowing that even she, at the tender age of eight, had a tradition. Probably had many more she was unaware of.

Her mood brightened and the awkwardness from before dissipated, and we rejoined the party in the living room. The last two guests had arrived, and you could have knocked me over with a feather at who it was. My wayward, difficult, ever-so-challenging, not to mention well-divorced sister, Rebecca Louise Duncan Samson Herbert. At her side was her latest boyfriend, whom I learned was named Rex, probably the first Rex I'd ever met, probably the last. Rebecca was ten years my senior and Rex was ten years her junior, making us the same age, yet he seemed even younger, aided by the presence of tattoos on his exposed arms. The two of them seemed a perfect match, because neither had yet to grow up. My sister kissed my cheek, Rex shook my hand, called me "Dude," and they both waved unenthusiastically when introduced to Janey.

"Where's Junior?" I asked my sister.

"With his father, the bastard," she said, though it wasn't clear to anyone listening—which was all of us—whom she was calling the bastard, the ex or her son. With my sister, you never know. Then, when she noticed Janey still clinging to my side, she apologized for her language. "Oops, sorry, not used to kids being around."

Great. Should be a fun afternoon.

Junior was her son by her first husband, he was ten years old, and frankly he would have been a nice playmate today (I had expected my sister to bring her son, not some dim boy toy), because I realized Janey was lost amidst this sea of adults. What did she have in common with this group of people? Four grown-ups who would talk money and business and gossip, my sister and her boy toy, and . . . me. Heck, maybe I could sit at the kiddie table with Janey, the two of us adrift in this rough sea. Rebecca went off in search of a drink, Rex followed her like a dutiful puppy, and when no one else was looking, Janey turned back to me and said, "Could we go and look at the Liberty Bell again?"

"It wasn't open the first time, Janey."

"I know," she replied, which had me stifling a laugh.

No one heard the exchange, busy were they with their own small talk.

We were a far cry from the gentle comfort of Linden Corners, and we found our homey farmhouse calling to us with desperation. I imagined Greta sitting down to a table filled with love, her four daughters and sons-in-law, their sweet children, the kind of Thanksgiving you saw perfected in television movies. What gave the Duncan family the illusion of perfection was the lushly decorated table, which now overflowed with food, a huge turkey that my father delighted in carving, "like a takeover, removing it piece by piece," he said, getting a hearty laugh out of a jovial Harry Henderson. There were also three kinds of potatoes and roasted chestnut stuffing and cranberries and rolls and warm crusty breads, vegetables, too, a feast to satisfy ourselves on. Good thing, too, as the conversation might have starved us.

My father and Harry talked business—stocks and the ups and downs of the volatile market—while my mother and Katrina talked about society gossip.

"Oh, that reminds me," Rebecca jumped in, deciding then and there was the right time to tell us how she had met Rex. She then related the story of a society function for a local hospital that was "dull, dull, dull, really, I could have died, except for the fact that I met good ol' Rexy."

"Yeah, that's what she calls me. Rexy. Getting me a leash for Christmas," said Rex. "Woof."

I thought my mother might keel over.

Janey giggled aloud. "Finally, someone else whose name sounds good when you add a 'y' at the end. That's how Brian and I met—at the base of our windmill, where I called him Brian-y and then said yuck. Brian-y. That doesn't sound good, does it?"

"Not in the least," said my mother quickly.

"What's all this about a windmill?" Katrina asked. "Sounds lovely."

"It was my mom's," Janey said. "It's really big, and it's beautiful, and Brian likes it, too, don't you, Brian? It has giant sails that turn in the wind and sometimes I imagine it spins stories, and I go there to hear them, because it's really my mom telling them to me. She always told me wonderful stories."

Janey's flurry of words suddenly quieted the table, adults looking around the table as though silenced by the profound. It was my father who broke the silence when he looked over at Janey and said, "Well, young lady, you must have inherited your mother's trait for telling stories, because I liked that one very much. Thank you, Janey, for gracing my Thanksgiving table with your very sweet presence."

"You're welcome," she said. "Thank you for inviting me."

"Anytime, Jane," my mother said. "You are just delightful. Sunshine in a storm."

Both of my parents caught my eye, and I mouthed a quick "thank you," even forgiving my mother her petty quirk of calling Janey "Jane."

"Oh, Brian, I forgot I have a hello to send to you," Rebecca said, taking command of the table again as though nothing of meaning had occurred. "I meant to tell you the moment I saw you, but I ran into Lucy Watkins at that same charity event where I met Rexy. She wanted to make sure I said hello."

"Who's Lucy?" Janey asked.

"No one," I said, and then with sarcasm added, "Thanks, Becs."

She shrugged, and for a moment it seemed the conversation had shifted.

Not so lucky.

"Lucy Watkins was Brian's first love—they dated all through high school and college, and it seemed like one day they would get married and I'd have a passel of grandchildren," my mother said. "I hear she has two children of her own now and that her husband is a doctor. She's done quite well for herself, Lucy has. I think her name now is Lucy Abrams."

Janey tossed me an odd expression that I couldn't decipher, and then whatever she was thinking, she dropped. And I let it go, too, and at last the conversation went down another path. The remainder of dinner passed uneventfully. All of us had our fill of food and drink, all of us were thankful for what we had, this feast and the company that enveloped us and the prosperity that surrounded us.

As the empty plates were cleared and dessert dishes were set at each place, my mother announced that this was the time for us all to announce what we were most thankful for. My heart sank. I had been hoping to spare Janey this annual ritual, thinking it might be a struggle for this girl who had lost so much this year to find anything to be thankful for.

"I thought we were beyond doing this kind of thing," I said.

"Brian, dear, it's a tradition, you know that, albeit slightly altered over the years." And she proceeded to tell the gathered crowd how this particular event had once upon a time preceded the meal, "until Kevin's repeated complaints about the turkey getting cold made us move it to dessert time. We used to have such large dinners, so many people were with us during a time when there was so much to be thankful for." My mother lost her train of thought and I sensed she was remembering Philip, which always left her flustered. She managed to recover by saying, "Rebecca always had so much to be thankful for, didn't you, dear?"

"I'll be short and sweet tonight," Rebecca offered.

"I'm always thankful for dessert," Janey said.

"Good," my mother said, "Jane got us off to a marvelous start. Anyone else?"

As we went around the table, I kept a careful eye on Janey, wondering if she had said all she wished to. After my father got his turn, stating how glad he was that his fortunes had prevailed this year, my mother went, saying how thrilled she was with her new house. Rebecca and Rex were thankful for finding each other, the Hendersons each following through with their own shallow thanks. Then all eyes turned to me.

"I'm thankful for the power of the wind, which blows through our lives and changes its direction, grateful that it dropped me in Linden Corners and at the base of the windmill. I'm thankful for the time I shared with Annie Sullivan, and mostly I'm thankful for her beautiful daughter, Janey, who, even when the sun doesn't come up, brings rays of light to my life."

"That was very nice, Brian, very, uh . . . heartfelt and poetic," my mother stated. "Now, who wants pie? I've got apple, cherry, even a peach pie—at Brian's request . . . oh yes, Jane, what is it?"

Janey interrupted my mother by raising her hand. "Don't I get a turn, you know, to say what I'm thankful for?"

"You did, dear, you were thankful for dessert. So, peach pie? I heard it's your favorite."

"Mom, let her speak."

The room again quieted down as Jancy found all eyes cast upon her. Her eyes flashed at me, uncertainty written in those irises. I gave her my hand in support, which she gratefully accepted. I squeezed once in another gesture of love. "I shouldn't really have any reason to be thankful, not this year. Awful things happened, terrible things that took from me the person I most loved, the only person I thought I could depend on. But maybe that was selfish thinking, because I know now that I'm really lucky, because I've got Brian, and even if he's not my real father, well, he's someone very special. He's my best friend, and I'm thankful that I get to share his . . ." She paused, looking at me, watching tears fall from my eyes as she smiled and said, "I'm just thankful I get to share his traditions and his family."

As we all settled in for pie and coffee, an enlivened, truly thankful gathering of people began anew. Because in that moment, a brand-new tradition began, a kinder, warmer Duncan Thanksgiving was born. The child among us had taught us a lesson we'd not soon forget.

CHAPTER 3

Janey was long asleep when eleven o'clock rolled around, exhausted from the emotion of the holiday, and stuffed, too, from a second helping of peach pie. I, too, was ready to turn in, since she and I planned to leave first thing in the morning. Good rest for a long drive. Though my place of employ in Linden Corners, George's Tavern, had been closed for the holiday, the weekend was understandably our busy time and I needed to be there for my customers. Yet there remained one more act of the performance that was the Duncans' celebration, and I found my parents asking me into the living room.

"Can't this wait?" I asked.

"We wanted to talk with you—a serious conversation, dear," my mother said, exchanging nervous glances with my father. "Please, have a seat."

I had been headed up the stairs already, but

the look on their faces had me retreating back, and again I found myself pulled into the living room, like a lamb to slaughter. Or turkey, considering the holiday. The fire had died down to embers.

"Okay, what's up?" I asked, rubbing my hands together. Not because I was cold.

"Brian," my mother began, "I have to confess, when you first told us what had happened up there in that town, and about that storm and that poor woman . . ."

"Annie, whom I planned to marry."

"Yes, sweet Annie," she said, as though she knew her, had met her, and had come to welcome her as part of the family. "We were worried about Annie having left the care of her precious daughter in your hands. After all, Brian, you became a city kid, a New Yorker who knows only about things like take-out meals and late nights out with your friends. What could you possibly know about raising kids? But seeing you with Jane today, how remarkable the two of you are together, I suppose we don't have to worry so much. I know I don't express my emotions very easily, I'm the first to admit that, but you're very good with Jane, patient and understanding."

"You listen to her," my father interjected. "That's important."

"Thank you, that means a lot," I said.

"Yes, well, given that, it only makes what we're about to tell you a bit easier," she said. "I know tradition is an important thing for you, that's why you were here today. Believe us, Brian, we know it and we appreciate it; so does Rebecca in her own uncommon way. We all remember . . . the family we once were. We also recognize that Jane must have her own way of doing things, and since Christmas is coming up . . ."

"What your mother is attempting to say, Brian, is this: We're suddenly faced with the idea of having our first Christmas without any of our children—we assume you'll be busy with Janey. Christmas is an important event in a child's life. As for Rebecca, well, who knows what crazy plan she'll come up with this year. Perhaps she'll buy Rex a doghouse—he certainly belongs in one." He paused, cleared his throat when he realized no one was laughing. "So, rather than spend a quiet and possibly remorseful holiday, we've decided not to be home for Christmas this year. We've scheduled a Caribbean cruise with the Hendersons. And though we were nervous about changing things up, I think maybe it's been a good decision. Now Janey can enjoy the holiday in her own home, with no pressure for you to join us for our way of celebrating Christmas. We hope you're okay with this."

I had said nothing during this exchange, letting them both speak their minds, prepared for the worst, comforted and soothed by their words, surprised, too. All day long I had worried that my parents had become fixated on the less-important parts of life, their money and their home, forgetting the wonderful things in life that you *could* take with you. Though no doubt they would spoil themselves on this upcoming cruise, the idea behind it, the selflessness surrounding their gesture warmed me. I found myself embracing them both, a scene as unlikely as any you'd find inside these historic walls. In a way, this new house of theirs became a home for me, too.

As we parted, I discovered the night wasn't over yet.

"We have something for you," my mother said.

Two more gifts awaited me, one I took with pleasure, the other with great reluctance. My mother had dug through the boxes of Christmas decorations and handed over a small, square box. Inside it was a shiny blue ornament, my name written across it in silver, glittery lettering. When I held it in my hands, a lump lodged in my throat. In my need to take care of Janey, I had forgotten about this lovely holiday trinket and a feeling of guilt washed over me.

"Thank you, thank you for remembering to give this to me," I said. "It means . . . so much. I will, of course, put it on the tree Janey and I decorate."

Nothing further needed to be said. Everyone in the family had one of these name ornaments, and every year I had hung mine on my parents' tree.

"Take a picture, please, and send it to us," my mother said.

Afterward, sniffling slightly, she excused herself on the pretense of finishing up the kitchen work, leaving me alone with my father. He resumed his role as stalwart businessman as he proceeded to hand me a thin white envelope. "Raising a child is an expensive proposition,

Brian, and last I knew you didn't really have a dependable job. Oh, I know, you're running that tavern, but surely that's not enough, can't be nearly enough. Probably your savings are shaved down to the bone. And before you refuse our help out of some sense of pride or whatever, think about what matters most. Think of whom this money will benefit most."

I didn't protest, not then. I just slipped the envelope into my pocket without opening it, without looking at whatever amount my father thought overrode pride. Our meeting was over, and at last I went to bed, checking first on Janey, who was fast asleep in the room of photographs. My old high school self hovering above, a kid unsuspecting of the direction his life would take. I looked, too, at the graduation pictures of Rebecca and Philip, and then I gazed one last time at Janey. Then I went to my room. Only when I was behind closed doors did I open the envelope and look at the check my father had presented me with. I shook my head. I knew thoughts of what to do with the check would interrupt my sleep, and I was right. I slept fitfully that night, pretty much waking every hour on the hour.

When we said our good-byes the next morning, my father swung Janey around in his arms until she was laughing uncontrollably, my mother then pecking her cheek, saying, "Good-bye, Janey."

"Thank you, Mrs. Duncan. I had a very nice time."

My father pecked her on the cheek and finally released her.

I think it was a difficult thing for him to do.

Despite the generous check from my father, I think the richness of the holiday was left behind inside that town house. My parents waited on the top step of their porch as we made our way down the ice-encrusted sidewalk to my car. I brushed any lingering snow from my windshield, tossing a small snowball Janey's way.

"Hey, not fair!" she said, but she laughed.

Then, as she piled into the car, I put the suitcases in the trunk. But one package I kept with me was the precious box with my family Christmas ornament inside it. I set it on the backseat for safekeeping. Janey grew curious about it and so I told her she could take it out of the box, but carefully.

"It's very valuable," I said.

"Oh, wow, Brian, it's so pretty," she said, her eyes sparkling against the blue glass as the ball twinkled and twirled in the sunlight. I let her admire its beauty, but when I put the car in gear, she knew to put it back in the box. "I'll take good care of this, Brian, your own ornament for our tree. Right, we will be having Christmas in Linden Corners?"

Through the rearview mirror my eyes settled once again on the ornament. Memories of Christmases past flooded my mind. "Yes, Janey, a snowy Christmas filled with wonderful new traditions."

CHAPTER 4

"Okay, Cyn, I'll see you in about an hour, thanks."

I set the cordless phone back on the counter, glancing at the clock as I did so. It was two thirty in the afternoon and Janey would be home from school within the hour, coinciding with the time when I would need to leave to set up George's Tavern for the long night. This was the Thursday following our Thanksgiving visit, usually not my night to work, but the relief bartender I'd hired was running late and wouldn't arrive until around six. Not opening until then would cut into my reliable happy hour business. So I'd asked my neighbor and friend Cynthia Knight if she wouldn't mind coming over to the farmhouse to stay with Janey for a couple of hours; she'd readily accepted, as she so often did. Cynthia had been Annie's best friend and could always be counted on in a pinch.

In fact, without Cynthia and her husband,

Bradley, this new life of mine, caring for Janey, might never have been possible. Since the time of the terrible summer storm that had claimed our precious Annie, the Knights had been invaluable. Bradley, though he practiced tax law, had recommended an associate from his firm who handled family court issues, and a few weeks after Janey's eighth birthday, guardianship of her had been granted to me by the Columbia County Family Court down in the city of Hudson. It had been quick and surprisingly effortless. A short hearing, testimony from several of the residents of Linden Corners—Cynthia, Gerta, the gang at the Five O'Clock Diner, even Father Eldreth Burton over at St. Matthew's—had helped in my endeavor to keep Janey living at the farmhouse, inside the only home she knew, and not be forced to live in foster care. Annie had also left instructions behind, words that proved to be the most powerful testimony in our petition. The courts couldn't ignore the overwhelming evidence set before them, that Janey Sullivan and Brian Duncan were the perfect match of child and guardian. All of our friends had promised to help out, and all had more than lived up to their part of the bargain.

But the legal issue was only one matter, and a technical one, because the actual daily caring for Janey was an even bigger one. Eight-year-old girls were fickle. It had been frightening and rewarding all at the same time, and while I knew Janey was as happy as she could be, there were times that challenged us. Because life handed you curves. Because life never went as planned.

Since September, I had been trying to establish
a set routine for me and Janey, knowing how important it was for me to be around as much as
possible. I was awake each morning to get Janey
ready for school, and on the weekends I was
around all day, especially Sunday, which was the
one day the tavern was closed, one of the many
traditions I'd held on to after the death of its
former owner, George Connors, who had also
been Gerta's husband. When I worked the late
hours on Mondays and Fridays, Cynthia came
over in the afternoons and stayed with Janey,
and on Tuesdays and Saturdays, Gerta came
over and did the same. Wednesday and Thursday represented my time with Janey, days I made
certain to be home, morning, afternoon, and
night, believing an uninterrupted two-day stretch
would give us some needed level of consistency.
Today was the first day that our regular routine
would be broken, and I had to hope Janey
wouldn't object too much. She was usually good
about change, usually so adaptable.

After my quick call to Cynthia, I hopped in the
shower, since I was all sweaty from yard work.
Early snow and late falling leaves made for a
messy combination out back, and so while I
worked and while the windmill spun, I felt anxious for Janey's return from school. Maybe we
could get started on some Christmas decorating. Now, dressed and refreshed, all of our
plans would have to wait. I stepped off the porch
at three in the afternoon, the cool afternoon air
invigorating me as I walked to the edge of the
long driveway. I saw that the yellow school bus

was just coming to a halt in front of the mail-box. Janey hopped off, as did her friend Ashley, a classmate who lived across Linden Corners. Oh no. I suddenly remembered Janey's request this morning, asking if her friend could visit today.

I waved to the regular bus driver, and she waved back before driving off to her next stop.

"Hi, Brian," Janey said.

"Hi. Hello, Ashley."

"Hi, Mr. Duncan," she replied, her brown pig-tails bobbing from the bounce in her step.

"So, what are you girls planning to do today?"

"It's a secret," Janey said.

"Yeah, secret," Ashley said in an annoying singsong copycat voice.

"Oh, so no boys allowed, huh?"

"Definitely not," Ashley commented, looking to Janey for confirmation. She nodded.

"Then you won't mind if Cynthia comes over for a couple of hours? Mark's going to be late for work, and I need to get the tavern set up."

Janey shrugged with uncharacteristic indiffer-ence. "Okay, no big deal," she said. She followed it up with a scrunch on her face. I knew what that meant. She had a question to ask.

"What is it, Janey?"

"How do you do that? Can you read my mind?"

I laughed. "If only. So, what's your question?"

"Can I show your pretty blue ornament to Ashley? I was telling her about it and how I wished that I . . ." She didn't finish her state-ment. "Can I?"

I said okay, but reminded her . . .

"I know, I know, be careful. I will, thanks. Bye."

And then she and her pigtailed friend went dashing up the driveway, where on the front lawn they saw one of the giant piles of leaves I'd worked so hard to gather. The two of them leaped into one of them, spewing crisp yellow leaves all over the lawn. I informed them that when they were finished they could find the rakes in the barn. Ashley stuck her tongue out at me. Gee, sweet kid. I hoped she wasn't too bad an influence on Janey.

Cynthia Knight arrived a few minutes later, walking over the hill that separated her farm from the Sullivan farmhouse, bringing with her a fresh bag of apples. As the local purveyor of quality fruits and vegetables, Cynthia managed a little stand on the outskirts of town, while her husband, Bradley, worked as a lawyer up in Albany. The two of them were a nice couple in their early thirties. I couldn't imagine my life without either of them.

"Thanks, Cyn, I owe you one."

"No debts here, remember?" Cynthia had an easy smile, which today highlighted her apple cheeks. Her long mane of blond hair was covered with a knit hat, and her entire body was wrapped in a warm jacket. Even still, nothing could cover up her big heart.

"Sure, right," I said. I'd heard it before. "If I'm going to be later than seven, I'll call."

As I hopped into my car, I called over to Janey.

"What's up?" she asked, breathless from her quick dash.

"Did you just say 'What's up'?"

"Ashley says it all the time," she informed me.

"Well, how about next time you try, 'Yes, what is it, Brian?'" Annie had been a stickler for Janey speaking properly, full sentences and polite demeanor, and usually that's just what you got. Not so today. I was trying to keep alive the same rules. "So, you okay with this? With me going to the tavern? This is usually our time."

"It's okay, Brian, I understand that you have your life, too," she said; then, without knowing if she was dismissed, she bounded off to the backyard, Ashley chasing after her but unable to catch up. It was amazing how quickly Janey could run from things, the distance between us so far, so fast, maybe more than I realized.

Since returning from the visit to my parents', I had begun to notice a slight change in Janey's behavior. Nothing drastic, just little actions or phrases or turns of the head that if you wanted to scrutinize could indicate a slight crack in our delicate foundation. Picking out her own clothes, wanting to fix her own breakfast in the morning, refusing help on her math homework, and now a noticeable indifference to my breaking our well-established routine. Maybe it was just the giddy excitement of having her friend over, but I was left with a feeling that Janey was somehow trying to assert her independence. As though my presence wasn't always needed. The idea that the sweet and innocent Janey Sullivan might outgrow me, tire of my care, hit me like a stake to the heart. Usually those sorts of paranoid fantasies tended only to penetrate my thoughts in the late hours, and here they were, coming to me during the daylight, creeping ever closer.

I headed to town, my stomach nervous and unsettled.

Worrying could come later. For now, as Janey had said, I had my own life to lead.

CHAPTER 5

Linden Corners was a tiny village located in Columbia County, New York, a hop and a skip from the mighty Hudson River, boasting a population of just over seven hundred people. Route 23 was the main road that cut through the downtown business district, where small shops and even smaller restaurants lined each side of the street. A small park that was rimmed by trees, highlighted by a white-trimmed gazebo in the center of its green lawn, helped keep the quaintness in Linden Corners. Just down the road was St. Matthew's Catholic Church, a cemetery adjacent to the old building and its towering steeple. Up one of the side roads was the Methodist Church, and in nearby towns Hillside and Craryville were other places of worship, along with even better services, fancier dining establishments, and antique stores that tended to cater to the renowned tourist trade. In Linden Corners, we liked to think of ourselves as self-sufficient, able to meet the needs of all residents, from Marla and Darla's Trading Post and Groceries, to Chuck Ackroyd's Hardware Emporium and Martha Martinson's Five O'Clock Diner; and of course, across from Ackroyd's, the formerly named Connors' Corner, now rechristened simply as George's Tavern. It was George's establishment I was most familiar with. Once the early home of George and Gerta, they had expanded as their family had, later turning the main floor into a bar, keeping the upper floor as an apartment. I had lived there when I'd first come to town.

With Thanksgiving having slipped by, the calendar had turned to December. So many of the townsfolk had begun to decorate their buildings with colorful lights and adorn their windows with Christmas pictures and banners and white frost, lighting up the village for the holiday season that had suddenly crept up on us. As early evening began to descend over the sky, I was reminded that I needed to do something festive with the tavern. I couldn't be outdone by the old-timers, not with this being my first holiday here. Approaching the building, I made a mental note to ask Gerta where George might have kept any decorations he'd used. I pulled into the parking lot adjacent to the tavern, getting out and waving across the street to Martha Martinson, the stout, fiftysomething proprietor of the Five-O. She served the best food in town. But today she'd traded her chef hat for maintenance worker. She was up on a metal ladder, hanging her own string of lights.

"Better hurry with that," I said. "It's getting darker earlier."

"Just looking at that lonely bar of yours over there, that'll darken any holiday this side of Halloween," Martha said, her good nature and humor intact, typically off-kilter.

The Five-O was so named for its peak feeding times, a.m. and p.m., and for me it held a dear place in my heart. It was just about the first place I'd ever stopped at in Linden Corners—the windmill notwithstanding—and both Martha and the waitress, a young girl named Sara, had welcomed me with unaccustomed friendliness. They had ended up changing my life, all for the good. My lunchtime visit became an overnight stay and then I stayed another night, and soon after found myself with a newfound job, and now months later, I was still here. All of it I took to be evidence that I was meant to be drawn in by the power of this unique village, by its residents, and by the windmill that seemed to speak to and inspire them. It had done so with me, still did.

Martha was right, the bar did look abandoned. I heeded her advice and hurried up the steps, unlocked the door, and immediately flicked on the overhead lights. Yellow beams illuminated the large room. I turned on the jukebox and the television that hung over the bar, turning on a sports channel. A mindless soccer match played in the background. In short order I had transformed the quiet building into a welcoming beacon off the highway. My relief bartender, Mark, had left the place in good shape from the night before, but still I went through my routine, cleaning the tables and wiping down the chairs and the long oak bar, too, polishing the side brass with a sense of pride that I'd learned from longtime owner, George. I checked the taps to make sure they were working, beer being the bread and butter of my business. Everything was in working order. I was ready for my first customers.

The sun went down early this December day, and by four thirty a shadowy dusk had settled over Linden Corners. Headlights flashed by as the early rising residents returned to the comfort of their homes for the night. Fortunately, a few of them stopped off for a drink, and by five o'clock many of the bar stools were taken. Cold beers were laid out in front of them, with a couple of the guys already asking for refills after their hard day's work. A young couple had arrived, as well, opting to take a table, and when I served them their drinks I set a bowl of well-salted pretzels in front of them. Keeps them thirsty, another trick of George's.

So all was under control at the tavern, nobody needed anything right now. I was able to take a breather, a chance to appreciate this still-new world of mine. Janey's comment about my having my own life again popped into my mind and I wondered if there was any truth to that. Since September I had felt that my life—my goals, my ambitions—was on hold, as I focused all my concentration on Janey. She needed it and I wanted to. After three months of the same, I had no doubts that I was doing the right thing. I had made a promise to Annie and another to Jancy, and given the circumstances I was happy to fulfill them, wishing still and always that the circumstances weren't what they were. Annie should be with us—today, yesterday, tomorrow, sharing the joy we tried to find in each little moment of every day. Instead, Janey and I survived together, my routine dictated by hers, certainly a big change from where I'd been even a year ago. Living the big life in New York, obsessed with its frenetic pace, its lures of the good life, and its tempting, false seductions.

My reverie was interrupted by the arrival of another customer. She was the waitress from the Five-O and not one of my regulars. Guess she had finished her shift over there. I said hello, asked her what brought her here.

"Hi, Brian. I was looking for Mark," she said, sidling up to the bar.

"He's running late," I said, curiously suspicious why she was asking after Mark Ravens. "Guess you're stuck with me, that okay?"

She shrugged. "Guess I'll have to live with it."

Lots of guessing going on, no one committing to anything. Or was that really true? Sara, a pretty blonde who wore a bit too much lipstick, was twenty-two, a lifelong Linden Corners girl, and unlike many of her classmates, she didn't seem eager to leave town. She liked her job at the diner, liked her friends, and from what I gathered from her expression now, she liked my relief bartender. She kept looking back at the door to see if he was coming through it.

"He should be here soon, why not have a seat."

"Thanks. Gimme a Coors Light."

"Watching your girlish figure?" I asked.

"No one else is," she replied, chuckling as she did. "Martha would have liked that one."

Martha and Sara, in addition to serving the best food in the area, both liked to joke around. Sara's humor was improving, since when I first met her our conversation had been laced with roadkill remarks, not exactly what you wanted to hear from a waitress at a small town diner. After all, the highway was real close.

"The Five-O looks good," I said, pointing out the window. Martha had finished putting up the lights and the perimeter of the diner was glowing with holiday lights, reds and greens and blues enlivening the bustling activity at the diner. It was, after all, just past five in the afternoon, the dinner rush.

As Sara sipped at her beer, the rim now stained with the faint kiss of her lipstick, I asked why she wasn't working. She explained how Thursday was her one day off all week, "which stinks, really, since it's one of Mark's busy days."

I nodded. "Didn't know you and Mark, uh, knew each other's schedules so well."

She easily grinned, and I needed no further indication she was smitten with him. "Yeah, well, I'd seen him around town, in school and stuff, even though he was a couple years ahead of me. He never gave me the time of day, not until I brought him over a dinner plate a few weeks ago. It was a slow night both here and at the diner, and so I did the neighborly thing. He invited me over for a drink after my shift ended, and I did, and, well, we've gone out a couple times."

"Good for you."

"You know it," she said with sudden confidence.

I laughed before I pushed off to serve another customer.

Mark Ravens was a local kid who worked during the day down in Hudson, waiting tables himself for one of the finer resort hotels, but he'd been looking for some extra cash around the same time I'd been looking for a relief bartender. His uncle, Richie Ravens, who ran the Solemn Nights Motel in town, had recommended him. One meeting was all it had taken. He seemed very responsible and mature, grounded for a guy his age. We shook hands, agreed on the hours, and ever since then bar receipts had picked up on the nights he worked. Point of fact, he was handsome and managed to bring in the ladies, evidenced by Sara's presence here tonight.

I refilled a couple more glasses and then, encouraged by the decorations up at the Five-O, I phoned Gerta Connors.

"Hello, dear," she said. "How's Janey tonight?"

Fine, I said, but also explained how I was at the bar, which gave me the perfect opening to ask after Christmas decorations for the tavern. Turned out that George did have some; he kept them in the attic of their home. "Do you want to come over some night soon and look for them? I'm afraid I can't venture up into that musty attic, not by myself anyway."

"Wouldn't dream of asking you. How about Sunday?"

"Perfect. Come for dinner, bring Janey," Gerta insisted.

I thanked her and hung up. Sara was still nursing her beer, still looking at the door. Her wish came true at five minutes after six as the door finally opened with the man she wished to see. With a blast of wind, in walked my relief bartender. Mark Ravens was just a couple inches shorter than me, five ten, and at twenty-four he grew his wavy dark hair long. Today he was sporting an unshaven, scruffy look. He smiled widely at the sight of Sara, then apologized to me for being late.

"One of the evening waiters didn't show up; they needed me to stay and at least set up for the dinner crowd. I took a few orders, too, and then he showed. Got some extra tips, which is always good for the holidays, right?"

"No problem, Mark. Things happen. Cynthia's with Janey," I said. "But, speaking of the ladies back at the farmhouse, now that you're here I'll hand over the reins to you and head on back." I wondered if Janey had eaten dinner yet. I knew I hadn't. "Hey, Sara, what's the Five-O special tonight?"

"For you? Braised roadkill, with a side of me," she said.

"I'll pass," I said. "On both." I snickered.

"Hey!"

"Fear not, I'll take the side," Mark added.

"She's all yours," I said. "Bye."

"Your loss, my gain. See you later, Windmill Man," Mark said, tying an apron around his waist while he leaned in for a kiss from Sara. "Hey, babe, I missed you."

Just a couple of dates?

A few additional cars had turned in to the tavern's parking lot. Several more ladies joined the action that was fast becoming a town attraction, George's Tavern on a Thursday night. Careful, Mark, don't let the single gals catch you smooching someone else in public. Receipts would go down real fast. Still, this bar, it just might make some money and maybe I wouldn't need that check from my father. I'd stashed it—uncashed—in a desk drawer, preferring to forget about it. I forgot about the bar, too, for now, leaving my business in capable hands. With a smile on my face, I was glad to know that Mark and Sara had found each other. Linden Corners needed a breath of happiness, a warm front sweeping down to remove the chill that had settled over the land this season. Little did I know just how cold it was going to get.

CHAPTER 6

When I arrived home, the farmhouse was unusually quiet. Ashley had thankfully already gone home, and Janey was upstairs in her room, doing her homework. I found Cynthia sitting on the sofa, a cup of tea at her side. She was knitting what looked like a small hat. Sometimes at the family fruit stand that she ran she sold homemade goods, both food and crafts. With the holiday season upon us, I supposed she was making gifts to sell.

"Looks nice," I said, indicating her handiwork.

She stuffed it into the nearby bag, yarn and needles and all. I'd obviously caught her by surprise, but why she was acting like I'd caught her hand in the cookie jar, I didn't know. But I didn't pursue it. "Oh, that, it's nothing really. Sorry, I didn't even hear you come in. All's well at George's?"

"Seems better without me," I said.

"So I've heard."

"Oh, local townsfolk gossiping about my old bar?"

"Starting to attract clientele from Hillsdale, I hear."

"Whoa, might have to break out the white tablecloths," I said. "But, yeah, as I was leaving, a gaggle of girls was heading inside. But from what I saw, Mark Ravens has his hands full with our Little Miss Sara from the Five-O." I laughed. "Listen to us, a couple of old biddies talking about the nonsense those kids are up to. So, how was Janey tonight?"

"Fine, as always," Cynthia said. "Had dinner around five thirty with Ashley, then her mom came and picked her up. I helped her with some math—and then she pushed me to do her reading. That girl could convince a cloud to shine. You know I would have called if there had been anything wrong."

"Her mood? Attitude, no problems?"

"None. Why? Brian, what's going on?"

Maybe nothing, I thought, dismissing my concerns as pure paranoia. "Forget it," I said. "Just tired, I guess."

"Me, too," she said.

Still, Cynthia seemed unconvinced, but she let it pass as quickly as I had her knitting. She knew that I'd open up if there was truly something seriously amiss. It wouldn't be the first time. I'd often sought her counsel when it came to the changing tides of an eight-year-old girl's current. Cynthia gave me a quick hug, then said she'd better get back on home. "Bradley was working late but he's probably home by now. I hope he started dinner. Gotta love the modern man. See you."

"Thanks, Cyn."

I went up and said hi to Janey, who waved at me without looking up, her face buried in her reading material. When I asked if she needed help, she just waved me away without even bothering to look up. Must be a good book. Feeling dejected, I went back downstairs and tooled around for another hour, until Janey's bedtime arrived. When I returned to her room, she was already in her pajamas, under the covers, still reading that book. Her stuffed purple frog was on one side of the blanket, a new plush puppy on the other. Glad she had such creatures to give her comfort during the night.

"Did you brush your teeth?"

"Of course, Brian. I know how to get myself ready for bed."

"I know. I just like to check anyway, okay?"

Her mouth quivered, just a slight tremor in her façade.

I sat down on the edge of her bed, feeling like a stranger all of sudden. Janey had been acting so grown up this past week, but now I saw that sweet little girl I'd met at the base of the windmill emerging, the one who'd been afraid of nothing. Not even a stranger. I wondered if something was frightening her, and I asked her if everything was okay.

"Yes."

She'd answered too quickly.

"You'd tell me otherwise?"

"Yes, Brian, of course I would," she said, her usual exasperation with me missing. Tonight her voice contained a noticeable distance.

"I love you, Janey Sullivan," I said, my voice suddenly failing me as a lump lodged in my throat. I waited a moment at the door, cleared my throat, then said with more confidence, "Good night, Janey. Don't forget to turn out the light when you've finished reading to your animals."

As I readied to leave the room, she called out to me. I turned quickly, hoping that whatever was bothering her was about to be revealed.

"Who was Lucy?"

"Lucy? Who's that?"

"You know, the woman you almost married. Remember, your sister talked about her at Thanksgiving."

"Just an old friend, really. Why, what about her?"

"Did you love her?"

Oh boy. Let the fun begin. This was not something to be dealt with in the frame of her door. I returned to her side, resuming my spot on the edge of the bed but not getting too close. The time it took to settle in gave me a chance to think up an answer to her unexpected question. "Her name's Lucy Watkins. What she and I had, well, that was a long time ago, when I was just a college kid and so was she and we didn't know any better. I didn't know what true love really was."

"Do you know all about love now?"

I smiled at her when I said, "You bet I do."

"Brian?"

"Yeah, sweetie?"

"Why did you come to Linden Corners?"

Why. Simple question, big answer. I hadn't even been able to answer it when Annie had asked me that very same thing. Did I even know how to answer it for myself? Sometimes you don't know why you do things, you just follow your instinct, follow the path that destiny has laid out for you. But neither of these arbitrary answers would suit Janey, and so I said to her, "You want to know the God's honest truth, Janey? I really don't know why I came to Linden Corners. I had never even heard of the place until, well, until I practically drove right through it. I might just have if not for your windmill." I paused. "You want to know another truth? A question I can answer?"

She nodded.

"I do know why I stayed."

This time she smiled and no more words were needed.

I was getting ready to leave again when she announced, "Ashley liked your ornament, Brian. I showed it to her after we raked up those leaves we made a mess with. She said she wants to see it again when we put it on the Christmas tree. Is that okay?"

"Sure, that's fine. I'm glad she liked it," I said. "You put it back in the attic with the other decorations?"

She didn't look at me, instead focusing her attention on the purple frog. "See what I have to put up with?" she told him.

I laughed, then gave Janey a kiss on the forehead.

"Back at ya, kid," I said.

On my way out, I turned off the light. No more books, I said, time for sleep. She accepted my decision without complaint, sliding beneath the covers and closing her eyes. I stared at her for maybe a minute, just watching her breathe. Wondering what was really going on in that mind of hers.

At last I retreated back to the living room, more confused than ever. For so many weeks, bedtime had gone smoothly, she and I talking any problems out with ease, with little riddle to our conversations. Tonight, though, Janey had knocked me flat with her questions about Lucy, a girl I'd not given any thought to in so many years. I'd had other girlfriends since Lucy, I'd endured several different phases of my unexpected life. But in the end I suppose it wasn't Lucy she was actually curious about. Maybe it was the discovery that there had been someone in my life before her mother. To Janey, it was like I hadn't really existed in the world until that day I'd appeared near the windmill. Realization was dawning on her that Brian Duncan had once led a different life. And it had been one that didn't include her.

CHAPTER 7

Saturday night I kept the tavern open longer than usual, until two a.m., and there was a good reason for it—there was nothing waiting for me back at the farmhouse. Janey had asked to have a sleepover at Ashley's and I saw no reason why not, so off she went with her overnight bag and off I went to a full night of work at George's. It was a busy night, with my regulars outnumbered by a group of out-of-towners who were here for an antiques holiday gift-buying exhibit. Regardless of who was from where, they were all looking for something to occupy their time for a few hours, a place where they could leave their troubles behind and celebrate the season. Apparently they had either lots of time to kill or lots of problems to forget, because as midnight came and went they all remained.

"You don't mind, where we come from, bars don't close till four," said a man about fifty. He didn't give off the impression that he'd closed many of those bars lately.

"Let me guess, New York," I said.

"Ever been there?" he asked.

"Called it home once upon a time," I said, feeling like it had been a million years ago, not just earlier this year. "Tell you what, I'll keep the taps going till two. Hopefully that will give you a taste of home."

"Good of you. We all need a taste of home, no matter where the world takes us," he said. "So, buy you a round?"

I shook my head. "Thanks, no. Like to keep a clear head."

"Bartender who doesn't drink."

I shrugged. "It's a business."

The taps kept up with the festive crowd, until one forty-five, when I announced last call. When they left, they gave a generous tip and wished me a happy holiday. Finally, the last straggler, one of my regulars, finished his beer at two fifteen, and as he ventured out into the cold early morning air, I locked the door behind him and set about cleaning up the bar. A half hour later I turned off the lights and left. George's Tavern was closed until Monday at four p.m.

Linden Corners was quiet as I drove along the empty roads, my headlights guiding me in the darkness. There was a noticeable chill in the air. Snow was in the forecast, along with some bitter cold, just as it had been for most of the last couple of weeks. Folks up in these parts liked the joke that there were two seasons in Upstate New York: winter and August. Gallows humor, I supposed. Still, aside from some harmless flurries, nothing of substance had accumulated today. The weatherman continued to spout those same predictions each night, I guess figuring he'd be right eventually.

I was about to make the turn off the main highway onto Crestview Road and head home. Instead I continued straight on Route 23 until I saw the mighty old windmill. The headlights of my car caught sight of the sails of the windmill, which were anything but dormant in these early hours of the new day. The wind had picked up the past couple of hours, was rushing across the open land like it wanted to be anywhere but here. Like I had often done during my first few weeks in Linden Corners, I pulled to the side of the road to get a better view of my favorite village landmark. Keeping the beams of light focused directly on the windmill, I hopped atop the roof of my car. Annie had called it Brian's Bluff, a direct response to a place along the river she'd shared with me, which I had dubbed Annie's Bluff. We had had such a short amount of time together, but time enough to reveal deep emotions, hidden places in the world and in our hearts. I gazed forward, wrapping my arms around myself for warmth.

And then I thought. I thought about the holidays and I thought about traditions and I thought about Janey, my thoughts always consumed with what was best for her. I thought about tomorrow, which was already today by the evident turn of the clock. Janey and I had planned to spend the entire day together, a typical, uneventful Sunday for us. But thinking, too, would it really be so typical? Our time together of late had been anything but. I thought about what we might do, what I might say, to somehow bring us back to the even footing that had been the foundation of our relationship. She had showed me so much with her big open heart. Heck, she'd even melted my parents' hearts, no easy feat. I thought of Kevin and Didi Duncan, wondering if their cruise was really a fresh start for Christmas, or were they just running from memories? Was I guilty of the same? Family was delicate, easily broken, like an icicle in strong wind.

The chill began to seep beneath my outer clothes and prickle at my skin, and I thought maybe I was thinking too much. I'd been guilty of that before, many times. The holidays did that. What if? What if things had been different? A guessing game no one could win. Silently, I said good night to the windmill, which really was a good night to Annie, watching as the snowflakes began to drift down right then and there, caught in the glow of the headlights. The strokes of a winter portrait appearing right before me.

When I returned to the farmhouse, I didn't turn on any lamps, the faint light from the shadowy moon outside filtering in, guiding me. I made my way through each room with easy familiarity, a sign that I'd become comfortable within these once-foreign walls. I changed into sweats and left my bedroom, taking a moment to look in at Janey's empty room. Her purple frog sat on the freshly made bed. He looked so lonely. Closing the door, I retreated back to the warmth of the living room. No television, no music, no noise, just the quiet sounds of night. I found myself staring out the window. It was snowing heavily now, and if this continued there was a good chance of waking to a blanket of snow covering the open land.

I tossed a blanket over myself and again my mind toyed with my emotions. In the wake of Annie being gone, visiting with her spirit at the base of the windmill generally brought me solace. Tonight it hadn't. Janey's lovely, alluring, headstrong momma had evaded me, almost as though she was siding these days with the emotions of her fickle daughter. An image of Annie's late husband, Dan Sullivan, popped into my head, and I wondered whether his spirit moved, did he ever visit the place he'd called home? Janey hadn't known him; she rarely spoke of him as she did her mother. Still, he had been her father. Father, capital letter.

No matter what else happened between me and Janey, good or bad or somewhere in between, there was no denying the truth. I was an impostor inside this home, a substitute for the people who had brought her into this world and given her life. Two people who had, in a moment of consuming, passionate love, made her the magical girl she was. At Thanksgiving Katrina Henderson had made a misjudgment by calling me Janey's dad. Maybe I had made the bigger mistake, thinking I could possibly fulfill that duty, if not in name then in spirit.

At last, I closed my eyes and drifted off to sleep, the first time I'd ever slept alone inside the Sullivan farmhouse. Ironic, no, that there was not a Sullivan to be found within its walls.

CHAPTER 8

Eight inches of fresh white snow had fallen by morning, and thanks to a wave of cold air that continued to flow past the countryside none of the snow threatened to melt. It was here to stay, just as much as the cold temperatures and the winter months. In fact, the top layer of snow was crunchy as our heavy boots stomped over it, an icy coating on top that made for treacherous walking. Janey and I had decided to take full advantage of winter's loud arrival, having dragged the red sled out of the barn—dusting it off after three dormant seasons—and then making good use of the steep hill located at the edge of the backyard. Janey's face was alive and happy from the fun she was having, the sled easily cutting through the wind as it raced downward. My job was simple: walk the sled back up the hill, just so she could go again. After about ten trips, I said, "Hey, when is it my turn?"

"Your turn? Brian, what do you mean?" she asked, her face masked by a hat and scarf. Still, I could see that famous querulous expression of hers.

"Come on, let me have the sled."

"Silly Brian. Grown-ups don't go sledding."

Like Trix cereal.

"Shows what you know," I said, taking hold of the reins of the sled. I climbed aboard it, trying to fit my six-foot frame on the red toboggan that wasn't made for me—for "grown-ups," as Janey had so sneeringly put it. Sitting upright first, my feet stretched far over the front of the sled's lipped front. Okay, that didn't work. Then I tried to sit cross-legged, but my knees were like wings on an airplane, unable, though, to take flight. Finally, I lay down on my stomach, my legs dangling over the back of the sled.

Janey found much to be amused about that position. "Brian, you won't get very far."

"Oh yeah?" I said, teasingly.

"Yeah."

"Watch this," was my final warning, and that's when I gave myself a good, hearty push. Suddenly, I was hurtling down the hill on a direct course with the windmill. Janey took up the chase behind me, her happy screams somehow giving the sled more power. Cold wind whipped at my face. I hadn't worn a hat. I decided the ride had gone on long enough and so I suddenly turned the sled over and allowed myself to crash into the piles of snow. The sled slid out from under me, easily continuing its journey after depositing its weighty cargo. As I rolled to a stop and feigned unconsciousness, Janey came up next to me. That's when I grabbed her ankles and pulled her down. She let out a quick yelp.

"Brian, stop, Brian, come on . . . ," she demanded in mock protest. As we wrestled in the hard-packed drifts, she grabbed a handful of snow and rolled it into a nice round ball. I got up to escape its wrath. She threw the snowball. It landed square on my chest, and, keeping the game alive, I fell to the ground like a soldier in battle. But this didn't stop the assault, as she continued to toss snowball after snowball at me. I buried my head with my arms, waiting for just the right moment to spring my surprise on her. Quickly, I grabbed a handful of snow, hurling it at her as I regained traction. She let out another peal of laughter while she retreated up the hill. I started after her.

"No, you have to bring the sled back up," she said as I closed in on her. "No fair, you're too big, you'll catch me easily."

So I let her have her way, because kids love to win. I went back for the sled, and while I did she managed to reach the top of the hill. When I returned, she planted another snowball on me, grabbing the sled as I ducked. In seconds she had leaped onto the sled and was making her escape down the hill once more, laughing as the distance between us grew. "Ha, ha, Brian, I won, I won."

See what I mean? Her victory was sweet for us both because it had been days since I'd seen her happy and smiling. And even though I was chilled to the bone, I wanted nothing more than for this moment of détente to last forever. I settled for another hour of winter playtime, during which we attempted to roll a snowman and he ended up looking like some winter creature instead, and finally we gave up. We went back inside the farmhouse to warm up. Her cheeks and the tip of her nose were a rosy red.

"Hey, Rudolph," I said, "how about some hot chocolate."

"Yeah, yeah, with real chocolaty sauce. And marshmallows," she said eagerly.

"I'll see what we've got."

"We always have them. Momma never lets us run out . . ."

In a flash, Janey had quieted down and run from the kitchen. I wanted to go after her, but decided not to press the issue. Not now, not after we'd had such a joyous time. Instead, I made the steaming mugs of hot chocolate, adding some Hershey's chocolate syrup to make it extra flavorful, as suggested. Letting it cool, I looked inside the cabinets and pulled out a half-empty bag of mini-marshmallows, probably left over from the summer. I tossed a bunch of them in each mug, and then brought them both up to her room on a tray that also had some cookies for dunking. Janey was sitting on the floor, leaning against the bed. I joined her.

"I'm sorry, Brian."

"You have nothing to apologize for. Janey, there's going to be a lot of times like that, you'll do something and suddenly you'll be reminded of your mother. I want you to remember them. I want you to talk about them. I want to hear all about them. Some of them will make you sad, but if you think about how much your mother enjoyed them, especially when you shared in her enjoyment, well, you'll start to remember all the wonderful times you had with her. Remember, you get to carry on her traditions. Like adding marshmallows to hot chocolate."

She sniffled. I reached for one of the napkins on the tray. She wiped her dripping nose, then took hold of the mug. She took a sip, then smiled.

"Mmm. Extra-chocolaty."

"You told me that's the way you liked it."

"Actually, that wasn't me," she said. "It was Momma who liked it with the chocolate sauce. And it's real yummy. Thanks, Brian. It's my favorite way now."

We sat in companionable silence as we sipped at our hot chocolate and emptied the tray of cookies, both of us even picking up the crumbs. I showed her how to get the maximum amount of crumbs by dampening her fingertips. Janey again informed me how silly I'd been to attempt to ride the sled. But she said it with a smile that belied her opinion. That only served to make the day even more special, knowing she and I had recaptured a piece of the magic that defined our relationship.

As she set down her mug, she wiped away a chocolate mustache. "Hey, Brian, can I ask you a question?"

"Anything, you know that."

"Are we going to get a tree?"

"A tree? You mean a Christmas tree? Of course we are."

"When?"

"When would you like to get it?"

"What day is it?"

"It's Sunday."

"No, the date."

"Oh, it's December fourth."

"In two weeks, I think. Momma and I, we would always go and cut down a tree in the middle of December, so we could have the tree decorated for a while. You remember I told you that at Thanksgiving? I like to see it all lit up, with that shiny stuff."

"You mean tinsel?"

"I don't think so." She paused, mused on the word. "No, that's not it."

"Icicles?"

"Yes, yes, the shiny strings!" she said. "I love how they look on the tree, but they sure do make a mess of the floor when you take the tree down."

"I call that messy stuff tinsel."

"Why are they called two different things?"

"I don't know. Sometimes the same thing has the same meaning, but has two words to describe it." I pointed to the near-empty mugs between us. "Hot chocolate is the same thing as hot cocoa."

"That's weird," she said.

"Yes, it is. At least we agree on calling our drink hot chocolate."

She was unconvinced still. "Now I'm not sure what to call them. Icicles or . . . tinsel. You and

Momma used different names. So that makes them different traditions."

Okay, how to handle this one? I gave it some thought, Janey just staring up at me as if I had magic answers floating above me, ready for the picking at the right moment. Parenting didn't work that way. "If you think about it, Janey, even though they go by two different names, ultimately it's the same thing, creating the same result. Tinsel or icicles by any other name would still produce a beautiful, glistening Christmas tree."

She thought about that. "Good one, Brian."

Phew.

"So, can we? You know, get the tree?"

"Of course, consider it done," I told her.

"Huh? Why should we pretend it's done? Where's the fun in that? Chopping the tree down is almost my favoritist part."

"It's going to take me a little while to get used to all your traditions, Janey."

"I can help."

"Oh yeah? How?"

"Follow me."

She left her room and padded down to the end of the hall, where she opened the door that led to the attic. Trailing behind her, I flicked on the lights to guide our way. It was cold up here, but Janey seemed impervious to it, so determined now in her mission that nothing could stop her. Amidst the sea of memorabilia that contained the Sullivan family history—and before them, the history of the defunct Van Diver

family, who had built the farmhouse and the
windmill—were several cardboard boxes marked
X-MAS in handwriting I recognized as Annie's.
Even deep in the attic, where the past came
alive, we felt her presence.

As I pulled the boxes from the tight corner,
Janey tore off the tops, revealing a burst of decorations, lights, shiny balls, and other trinkets
that would be set on the fireplace mantel or on
the walls or upon the doors. There was also an
envelope marked PICTURES, and when I opened
it I discovered they were photographs of a
Christmas past. Annie in her bathrobe, Janey in
hers, the two of them surrounded by gifts and
boxes and discarded wrapping paper. Janey
squealed in delight when she saw them, telling
me these were from last year, she knew, because
that's when she had gotten the sled, the one we
had been using today.

"See the sled in the background of that
photo . . . I remember, because last Christmas
there was no snow and so I couldn't use it that
day. I was bummed," she said. "I guess Momma
never had time to put these in a photo album.
Look, there's one of Cynthia and Bradley, they
came over last year, I remember that, too. See,
Bradley took that picture of Momma and Cynthia.
Cynthia's holding my new baby doll, pretending
to feed it its bottle. And that's me. . . ."

Janey and I sat there for a good long time,
poring over each photograph. I listened to the
stories that accompanied each one, making
mental notes to myself about ideas to incorpo-
rate into our upcoming holiday, the first we

would celebrate together. She returned the photos to their protective sleeve and resumed her search. She was clearly looking for something specific. Suddenly she grew excited again as she pulled the top off another box. She clapped wildly when she made her discovery.

"Brian, you'll love this, I know you will," she said.

She withdrew in her tiny hands what must have been Annie's most favorite Christmas decoration of all: a ceramic, brightly painted, snow-covered windmill, with sails that actually spun. Carefully, Janey handed it to me and I gazed lovingly on it, mesmerized by its transforming beauty. Like the windmill outside, like Annie herself. I asked Janey if we could bring this one downstairs now and she clapped at the suggestion.

"It's never too early for Christmas," she said.

"No, not in the land of the windmill it's not."

Just then the telephone rang downstairs, and Janey went racing to answer it, leaving me in the attic alone. I started to get up before changing my mind. I knew there had to be other photographs from years ago, and I wanted to see those. When I found them at the bottom of another box, I started to look through them, hunting for other clues to Christmases past. I stumbled upon an album that turned out to contain memories of Janey's first Christmas. She was just eleven weeks old, with Annie holding her as she sat in front of the Christmas tree. No doubt her husband, Dan, had taken the photo. As an answer to my question, the next photo was of Dan holding Janey, a smile brightening his handsome face. Emotion swelled within me, blocking my throat. My God, what forces of nature had brought this precious little girl to this moment, only eight and planning her future holidays without either of these people in her life. How fortunate I was to be caring for her, but how daunting a task it was, too. Was I really up to it? Suddenly feeling like I was an intruder to history I had no business knowing, I put the photo albums back in their box and tried to reseal the tape. It flipped open, as though taunting me. In that cold, musty attic that day, I made a vow—to Annie and to Dan Sullivan, too—that I would do all I could to make this holiday perfect for Janey. But how? I knew she would need the most special gift possible.

When Janey returned to the attic, she scrunched her nose at me. "Hey, come on, that was Gerta. We're having dinner with her, remember?"

I had remembered, but I hadn't realized how much time had gotten away from us. It was closing in on five in the afternoon. The farmhouse had darkened along with the outside world. I asked Janey to give me a couple more minutes to get organized. Something was amiss, or more accurately, something was missing from the attic. I had placed my family ornament in the near corner, by the staircase. Today, though, it wasn't there.

"Janey, did you show Ashley my ornament?"

"Yes, oh Brian, her eyes just lit up. Remember? I told you," she said. "You're very forgetful lately. I could see the blue glass in her eyes, that's how pretty it is."

"Where did you find it?"

She turned and pointed to the exact location where I had placed it. "Hey, where's the box?"

"That's a good question," I said. "Are you sure you didn't leave it in your room?"

Janey nodded, her lips starting to quiver. "Uh-huh. I put it right back there."

She was noticeably upset, and after the great day we'd had I didn't want to jeopardize her mood further. And so I said we should forget about it, it must be somewhere among the other boxes. Maybe I had moved it—after all, wasn't I the forgetful one these days?

"I'll find it later, Janey," I said, reassuring her, but not me. "No big deal."

CHAPTER 9

Gerta, it seemed, was having a busy Sunday. As I turned the car into the snow-coated driveway, the porch light was suddenly turned on, bathing two figures in a soft glow. Gerta was easily discernible, the man less so. His familiar figure was hunched over, and as he moved slowly down the steps, his face became visible. A quick embrace of Gerta, then he headed toward the other parked car in the driveway. I pulled in right beside his, shut off the engine. As I suspected, it was Father Eldreth Burton, the quiet-voiced, longtime pastor of St. Matthew's Church and a good friend of the Connors family. Actually, to most families within the friendly confines of Linden Corners, the Sullivans notable among them. Janey and I hopped out of the car just in time to say a quick hello.

"Ah, Miss Janey, and how are you on this fine snowy Sunday?"

"Fine."

"I didn't see you at mass today," he said, giving me a sidelong glance.

Jancy gave me one, too. Both of them looking to me for an explanation. Okay, my fault. Her sleepover at Ashley's had not included church, and frankly, I had forgotten. So I offered up an apology. "Next week, we promise," I said.

"Let's not forget the reason for this very giving of seasons," Father Burton said. "But I know how busy a time it can be, especially with young, excitable children. As long as we see you Christmas Eve for the children's pageant—wouldn't be the same without your smiling face, Miss Janey."

"Thank you, Father."

"Yes, thanks."

"Good night, Brian. Good night, Miss Janey."

The old pastor headed off, his taillights like glowing Christmas ornaments encased in the floating darkness. We went inside, out of the cold. Gerta greeted us with kisses, and then got us settled inside her comfortable home.

Gerta Connors lived on the far side of the village of Linden Corners, a good two miles away from the farmhouse, in a white clapboard house she had shared for nearly fifty years with her husband, George. It was a home that had seen four girls grow from infants to adults to parents themselves, all while surrounded by lots of love and some of the best cooking and baking I've ever tasted. Tonight was no exception, as Gerta prided herself on her home-cooked meals and her warm brand of love. As she explained, "I don't get much opportunity these days to whip up something special, so I welcome the chance to cook for others. I extended an offer to Father Burton, but he begged off, claiming another invitation, which may or may not be true."

"What was he doing here?" I asked, suddenly concerned. "Are you okay?"

"Of course, I'm fine, Brian. We were discussing the annual St. Matthew's holiday fund-raiser. George was such an early supporter of those events, and Father Burton wanted to know if this year I would like to be included. So kind of him. But that's for another time. For now, we eat."

She had made a turkey breast with stuffing and vegetables, and said for dessert there was a fresh-baked strawberry pie, her summer specialty and one of my new favorite sweets. Folks in Linden Corners, they knew their pies. Annie had learned her peach pie from Gerta.

"It's like Thanksgiving all over again," Janey said.

I think the choice of meal had been deliberate on Gerta's part. Upon returning from Philadelphia, I gave her the details of the Duncan family holiday, and as a result I think she wanted to give Janey a chance to celebrate a Thanksgiving meal in a place that was closer to her mother's heart. The only fact I had kept from Gerta was the monetary gift from my father. No one other than my parents and I knew about it, and I preferred to keep it that way. So, grace said, drinks served, we feasted on food and company and the welcome feeling of a blended family. After dinner I helped clean up, while Janey went into the living room to watch *Rudolph the Red-Nosed Reindeer* on DVD. That gave me and Gerta an opportunity to talk.

"How are you doing?" I asked, drying a pan.

"Oh, Brian, you know me. I get by."

"With a little help from your friends," I said, realizing such a sentiment applied to us both. "That's the good thing about Linden Corners, we can't help but look out for one another. I don't know what I'd do without you all, you and Cynthia and Bradley. Heck, even Mark—having him take some of my hours down at the tavern has made a huge difference. Janey and I, we need that extra time together."

"Of course you do," Gerta said with authority. "Now, Brian, be honest with me, are you making enough money at the bar, you know, to be paying Mark? I know you're not paying him a lot and you rely on tips a lot, but you've got such responsibilities now. It's not just the amount of time you spend with Janey, but how you can provide for her."

"Now you sound just like my father," I said, deciding it might be a good idea to share what he'd done for me. Get a second opinion on what I should do with all that money. "My father gave me a check at Thanksgiving, said it was his way of helping."

She nodded. Said nothing.

"What aren't you saying?"

"I don't want to know how much," she said.

"Yes, you do."

"Fine, I do. But not because the amount is important. It's the reason behind it."

"Twenty-five thousand."

"Wow—that's very generous."

"But I don't want to accept it, Gerta. I realize what a help it would be, but . . ."

She said nothing again. I hated it when she did that. She waited for me to answer my own question.

"I'll figure out what's right."

She pointed toward Janey. "You always do."

"Okay, but what to do about the check can wait until after the holidays," I said. "Then I'll start to figure out what the future holds. You know, New Year, new life, all that stuff about resolutions. Maybe this year it's time to make some and actually keep them. I've thought that I need to find myself some additional form of employment with more regular hours and better pay. The question daunting me is what to do—and where. Don't get me wrong, Gerta, I love running the bar, and I enjoy the sense of freedom it affords me. But in reality, it's probably not the most suitable long-term solution given the current circumstances."

Gerta finished loading the dirty dishes in the dishwasher, then poured soap into the dispenser. "Has Janey said anything about it?"

"No. But I'm not sure she would. Janey's a constant marvel; some days I'm amazed at how composed she is. Still, she's a kid and she reacts like one. If something's bothering her, she's more apt to shut down. She reacts by not reacting. Last night, she had her first sleepover since . . . since Annie died, and all night long, both at the bar and when I returned home, I couldn't concentrate on anything, not the customers or on falling asleep. Alone in the farmhouse, I never felt more like an intruder. I think part of me was waiting for the phone to ring, and it would be Ashley's mother asking that I come and get Janey. Or hoping it would ring. But the call never came, and I can't figure out whether I was glad or sad."

"I think you didn't like rattling around that farmhouse all by yourself."

"I kept the bar open until two a.m., got home after three."

"Oh, Brian. Avoidance never solved anything."

We had finished with the dishes and Janey was absorbed in the movie, so Gerta escorted me upstairs to the attic so I could find the decorations I'd originally come for. My second attic visit of the day, this trip went quicker because I was left to my own devices and easily found the cardboard box marked CORNER X-MAS. There was no history lesson behind its discovery. I carried the box downstairs and loaded it into my trunk, returning to the kitchen to find coffee and slices of strawberry pie set out on plates. Janey ate hers in front of the television--the movie headed into its final half hour. So I sat opposite Gerta at the kitchen table. I took that first bite, allowing the sweet berry flavor to burst inside my mouth, the luscious juice taking me back to the tastes of summer. Pictures flashed of the Memorial Day picnic that had signaled an upward change in my burgeoning relationship with Annie. Gerta noticed the smile on my face and said, "You're welcome." I had a second slice.

"You know, Gerta, I could use some help at the tavern tomorrow—during the daytime. Martha Martinson's been giving me such a hard time about the bar's lack of decorations, and I've got to get them up as soon as possible. Maybe you can show me the way George used to hang the lights. I want the bar to be decorated on the outside just like he did."

"If you like," she said, a surprisingly noncommittal response for her. When I called her on it, she confessed that too much of our lives were already mired in the past. That's why they call it tomorrow, she said. "So decorate the bar the way you want, Brian, it's yours."

"No, Gerta," I said, shaking my head. "I'm merely the barkeep. Hired help."

"You're not merely anything, Brian Duncan Just Passing Through."

I laughed at the mention of the old nickname I'd been given this summer. An ironic name for sure. "Hey, that name's been retired."

"Nothing's ever retired, Brian," she said, taking a sip of her tea. "Things, events, they just lie dormant, waiting for the right time to come back. Like spring, it'll be back."

"After a long winter."

"Yes. Winter's Just Passing Through."

"Like traditions," I said, my mind suddenly flashing back to my own family. My parents and their desire to spend Christmas away from their fancy new home. My sister, Rebecca, who seemed usually adrift during the holidays, running from relationship to relationship, the years passing but the men somehow growing younger. And what of myself—was I ready to leave behind all the traditions I had known, those that had helped shape me? I thought of the ornament that was mysteriously missing, and that unlocked in my memory bank pictures of my brother, Philip. He'd been the oldest of the three Duncan children, twelve years senior to me, an older brother to look up to. A championship athlete, he had had the world at his feet.

Gerta was right, as always, nothing goes away forever. Not things we think we lost, that we forgot. Certainly not memories, they rise back to the surface when you least expect them.

"You still with us, Brian?"

I looked up and found Gerta staring at me. "Yes, sorry. I was daydreaming."

Janey had just entered the kitchen with her dirty plate when she heard what I said. "It's nighttime, Brian, you can't daydream at night."

Gerta just chuckled. "Out of the mouths of babes," she said.

We did the last of the dishes and thanked Gerta for her warm hospitality and wonderful food, and then bade her good night. As we left her driveway, I paused, took a look at the quiet house. Gerta lived alone, a widow, and I hoped she found comfort in her solitude.

Janey and I returned home shortly after nine o'clock and she fell fast asleep, exhausted from our very full day and even fuller meal. I retired to the living room, where my eyes rested upon the bright, ceramic windmill I'd taken down from the attic. Again, my mind whirled with thoughts, not unlike a windmill's sails, thinking about Janey and about the wonderful day we had shared, about how the two of us had seemingly leaped over the hump that had impeded us this past week. And then I thought about Annie. I could feel her spirit with the mere presence of the windmill. I sat for hours, just thinking, planning, wondering. Always worried about the next day, anticipating what tomorrow might bring. It dawned on me that nothing ever goes as planned, not tomorrow, not holidays, not our lives or the lives of the children who inspire us. I had to just let things happen as they happened.

I flicked off the lamp beside the sofa, but I left on the small light inside the windmill. Annie's spirit, glowing against the walls.

That night, I slept better, feeling as though there were two Sullivans within these walls.

But only one Duncan.

CHAPTER 10

Even though I'd called the farmhouse home since September, my New York friend John Oliver never called me there, opting instead to phone me at George's Tavern. I had a cell phone, but it was really only used for emergencies. Linden Corners wasn't a bastion of modernity. John knew when he could catch me; usually the call came during the day while Janey was at school and I was doing upkeep at the bar. Which meant the company he theoretically worked for was picking up the tab for the call. He could talk for as long as he wanted. Ten o'clock that Monday morning, it appeared John had all the time in the world to spare. I'd just arrived at the bar, leaving the box of Christmas decorations on the bar to answer the phone.

"Corporate drone, that's all I am. They expect me to wake up after a whole weekend of partying and playing and just start working right away?

Clock strikes nine, get to work. I don't think so," John was saying, his usual mantra. When I offered up no response, he asked, rhetorically, "I mean, whatever happened to easing into your workweek? Checking the scores from the night before?"

I answered anyway. "Maybe you should ask them if you can have Mondays off."

"Nah, sounds good in practice, but that would only mean I'd have to go through the same ordeal every Tuesday," he said matter-of-factly. My friend, so practical. "Man, Brian, it's just mornings, they're killers. I can't imagine what it's like to get up to milk cows before the sun comes up. How do you do it, farmer boy?"

He was convinced that, because I lived in a farmhouse, I had chickens and cows and all sorts of barnyard animals running around. He had yet to visit me here, not that I had extended any invitation. Janey Sullivan was not ready to meet John Oliver, and vice versa. Still, it was nice to know John hadn't changed at all since I'd left New York.

We chatted back and forth for a good twenty minutes on any number of topics, and when things shifted to the week's coming forecast, I informed John that I had work to do. "Is there a point to this phone call?"

"You slay me, man. Can't a friend just call his friend? Okay, well, you got me. Look, I was wondering, am I going to see you this month? You know, are you coming down to the city anytime soon? I mean, it's been too long. We gotta go for some beers, like we always did."

Frankly, I hadn't given a trip to the city any

thought. I had closed the chapter of my life that was New York City months ago, and aside from occasional thoughts of its steel canyons and its crazy pace and its memories, both good and bad, the city that had once kept my pulse racing had faded away to life support. Another life, experienced a lifetime ago. Still, I had to wonder why John was asking about a visit. I decided a direct approach would get me off the phone faster.

"I'm in love," he announced.

Good thing I wasn't cleaning a beer glass when he made that pronouncement, or I might just be picking up shards of glass from the floor. "You want to repeat that? I think we've got a bad connection."

"Hey, it happens to you all the time, Bri, why not me?"

"Because you're the kind of guy who thinks love is a four-letter word."

"That part hasn't changed," he replied with a knowing smile I could somehow visualize.

"That's not exactly what I meant."

"Brian, you have no idea, she's amazing. Come on, drop on down this way for a weekend. We'll revisit all the old haunts, maybe even find you a nice girl . . ."

"You're forgetting one thing."

"What's that?"

"I've got a girl already. A certain eight-year-old named Janey," I said. "John, I can't just go running off to New York for a buddy weekend. I have responsibilities, people who count on me, and I'm not just talking about Janey. As it is, she and I only get one day a week to ourselves and that's precious time . . ." Suddenly a random thought popped into my mind, cutting off my own speech. I considered my idea quickly while silence ate up the phone line between us. Then I said, "What are you doing next Sunday?"

"This coming Sunday? I don't know, it's only Monday."

"Keep it free."

"Yes! We going barhopping?"

"Not at all. You say you're in love? I need proof, that's for sure. I want to meet this woman who has transformed your life. And John, I want you to meet the one who changed mine. Though mine is an eight-year-old girl who will charm your socks off."

"Mine charms off more than that," he said.

"Okay, no comment like that ever again. Please."

Still, John's juvenile joke reassured me that his proclamation of love hadn't affected his foul sense of humor. We talked a few more minutes about possible scenarios for the coming weekend's visit and then we signed off with a laugh, John getting in one last dig about the farmer lifestyle he thought I'd adapted to.

"I am not a farmer," I exclaimed into the phone. It was no use, he'd hung up already, no doubt already dialing another friend. Heck, it wasn't yet noon, how could he be expected to be working?

As for me, there was a lot of work ahead of me, notably the Christmas decorations to be hung around the outside of the tavern. I grabbed the box from the edge of the bar, headed out to the porch where I'd already set up the ladder, leaving the staple gun on the top step. Buttoning up against the cold air, I began the task at hand. There were plenty of lights, and after an hour's work I had barely made a dent in stringing them along the building's perimeter. An assistant would have been helpful, but Mark was busy at his other job today. I would have taken anyone at this point, as long as they had previous experience. Something I lacked. At one point I found myself tangled in a mess of wires and when I tried to clear myself, I only made more of a mess of the situation. In other words, I lost my footing on the ladder and fell to the snow-covered ground. Quickly I brushed myself off and resumed my holiday work, glad no one had seen what had just transpired. A few minutes later cars started to pull into the parking lot of the Five-O across the street. I realized it was lunchtime. I'd been working for a couple of hours. I put down the staple gun, locked up the tavern, and walked over to the diner, where I took a stool at the front counter.

"Hey, Brian, sorry you stopped putting up those lights of yours," Martha said, stifling a laugh, "though we did have to get back to work. You put on a good show—lots of comedy."

So much for no one witnessing my tumble from the ladder.

"Gee, didn't know you were that bored, Martha."

"Oh, anything for a laugh," she said.

"I know what you mean, I certainly don't come here for the cooking."

I heard a series of chortles from the other customers, from Sara, too, who was pouring me a cup of coffee.

"Good one, Bri," she said.

Martha, feigning injury to her chef's pride, turned her back to me. It wasn't often someone got the best of her and as good-natured as she was, she still wouldn't admit I'd finally gotten one over on her. She returned to the kitchen, and Sara put in my order for a cheese and mushroom omelet. Ten minutes later Martha emerged from the kitchen with a steaming plate of food and set it before me, grinning as she did so.

"Come on, Windmill Man, take a bite."

"Should I trust you?" I asked kiddingly. I ate anyway while Martha stood nearby, watching me.

After I'd taken a few safe bites, she leaned in and said, "So, Brian, you're setting up the Christmas lights just like George did; does this mean you'll be hosting the annual party, too?"

I chewed, anxious to get my question out. "What party?"

"Week before Christmas, George Connors would open up the Corner for any and all, play Santa to all us needy—and thirsty—children. Heck, it's a Linden Corners tradition. Gerta sets out a nice buffet, something I always appreciated since it gave me a day off from cooking. Can't tell you how many First Friday celebrations I was serving up meals at two in the morning after the close of his summer party. You drink a few, you get hungry, that's the way it goes. But the Christmas party at the Corner, it ain't Christmas without it."

"First I've heard of it," I said. "Gerta never said a word. I was just there last night."

Martha shrugged. "Who knows? We've seen a lot of change this year in our fair village, so maybe Gerta wants to move on."

I nodded, knowing exactly what she meant. We'd all lost people we'd loved, their deaths tragic, sorrowful, remorseful. And as difficult as loss was, at this time of year you couldn't help but recall them with a greater intensity. I was an expert at such feelings; it was part of the Duncan family, too. I wouldn't have expected Gerta to feel the same and was surprised that she had failed to mention the Christmas party to me. Wouldn't it be her way of remembering George by resurrecting one of his time-honored ways?

"Maybe a party is just what we all need," I said to Martha.

She nodded in agreement.

"'Tis the season," Sara said, refilling my coffee cup.

"Just don't say anything to anyone, not just yet," I asked them both.

"Not a word," Martha agreed.

"But if we don't tell anyone, how will anyone know to come?" Sara asked.

"For now. Let me do the telling," I said, explaining that I wanted to first run the idea past Gerta anyway. She might have had her own reasons for not speaking up about George's traditions. If she wanted to skip the party this year, I would respect her wishes.

I polished off my meal, leaving nary a crumb— "nothing for the mice," Martha liked to joke— and returned to the tavern, where, inspired by the spreading of holiday cheer, I attacked those darn lights with a vengeance. Before long they were all up, lining the porch and the outer trim of the old house. It had been a major undertaking, and thankfully I had accomplished it before the sun had gone down. I had an hour to wait, actually, before true darkness fell and I did so with great impatience, ready to see my handiwork brightly displayed. At four thirty, as night began to fall, the colorful lights went on across at the Five-O, at the bank, and down the street by Marla and Darla's Trading Post. Linden Corners was suddenly a burst of reds and greens and oranges and blues, silver, gold, a holiday rainbow that shimmered against a black sky. I was just ready to contribute to the village's holiday glow when a car pulled into the parking lot, tires crunching in the snow. It was Gerta.

"Oh good," she announced. "I'm not too late."

"I was just about to flick the switch," I told her. "Unless you'd like to do the honors."

"It's your bar," she said.

"So all decisions are mine?"

"Certainly, Brian."

I ran inside, quickly flipping the switch. Gerta's gleeful exclamation called to me. I dashed out, backing up to the sidewalk where Gerta now stood in full appreciation. So it was there that she and I admired the explosion of color that encircled

George's Tavern, reborn with the glow of a new life, new light.

"It's beautiful, Brian, like nothing has changed. See, it's just as we discussed last night, traditions cannot be denied. They take on a power all their own. You've brought back George's spirit, and I appreciate it so much. In fact, there's this other tradition George had . . ."

"And I hope you'll be able to make it," I said.

Gerta smiled and I hugged her. I sent a silent thank-you across the street Martha's way. It was true; everyone in Linden Corners seemed to look out for one another, and this was just one more example of our extended family hard at work. As the Christmas lights shed bright, colorful shadows upon the snow, a silver tear trickled down Gerta's cheek.

"The Corner Christmas party lives on. Oh my, Brian, I guess I have some cooking to do," she said happily, anticipation energizing her smile.

CHAPTER 11

Our good friends Cynthia and Bradley Knight lived half a mile away from the Sullivan farmhouse, just up Crestview Road on a farm of their own. They grew a wide assortment of fruits and vegetables and sold them (in season) at their stand located just on the outskirts of Linden Corners. It was Wednesday, just two days after I'd put up the decorations at the tavern, and I had been busy shopping for gifts. I had instructed Janey to go to Cynthia's after school, promising to pick her up when I was done with my errands.

"Why can't you wait till school is over and take me with you?" Janey had asked that morning.

"Because I'm going Christmas shopping," I said.

"Oh," she said, and tried not to giggle. She failed. "For me, yay, for me!"

Well, that was the truth, and by the time six in the evening rolled around, I thought I had accomplished a good deal. So I headed home, stopping at Cynthia's to pick up Janey. Bradley was working late and wouldn't be there for another two hours. I found Cynthia and Janey concocting a casserole in the kitchen, and I readily accepted the invite to dinner. We ate happily, Janey inquiring about my shopping spree. I remained mum. She didn't really want to know what I'd bought; she could wait. Still, she was an eight-year-old girl and thus had to act like one. Afterward, Janey went to the living room to watch television, leaving me a moment alone with Cynthia.

"Kids," I said, rolling my eyes. "What is it about Christmas with them?"

"You don't remember."

"I never had a kid before."

"Brian, I meant you. You were a kid once."

"Okay, good point. Yeah, I used to drive my mother crazy, I'd try and find all her hiding spots. One year I did, found my big gift stuffed in the back of the bedroom closet. Christmas morning was a total letdown," I said. "What about you, were you an impossible girl?"

"Let's just say my mother said she'd get her revenge one day."

I didn't understand and said so.

"When I have to deal with my own kids," she said. "You're kinda thickheaded tonight, aren't you, Bri? Everything okay? Something bothering you?"

I looked away a moment. Then I turned back and said, "Everything okay with Janey today?"

"Why wouldn't it be?"

Okay, might as well get her perspective and insight. "We've had a couple of difficult nights, that's all. A bit of attitude in her tone, asserting her independence. This coming holiday season, Cyn, I'm guess I'm just worried about her. She and Annie shared so much, I don't think I can possibly live up to their Christmas memories. And as much fun as I had today buying her gifts, they're just trinkets. The real spirit of the holiday may just elude us."

"Oh, that's where I think you're wrong," said Cynthia. She shushed me while she peeked around the corner. Janey was watching the lighting of the Rockefeller Center Christmas tree. "All day long, Janey kept asking me what she could get you for Christmas. Something special, she kept saying—her words. She was quite insistent. I had a quick doctor's appointment; Janey came with me. Then afterward we stopped at Marla and Darla's. Janey spent so much time in the card section, looking at ornaments and such. Oops, I promised Janey I wouldn't spoil the surprise . . . well, I haven't given anything away. Just don't go peeking inside her closet." She patted my arm. "Brian, you've done a remarkable job with Janey these past few months, and she knows it. So don't worry about Christmas. Just keep doing what you've been doing; that's the best gift of all."

So Janey had been looking at tree ornaments at the store. For a second I contemplated telling

Cynthia my fears about the missing ornament and then thought better of it. Explaining the situation would require explaining its significance, and I wasn't prepared to get into that story, not now.

So instead the three of us watched the remainder of the Christmas special together, Janey clapping at the ice-skaters, and once the big tree at 30 Rock had been lit, I gathered her into my arms and we left Cynthia's warm home. As Janey hopped into the car, I turned back to Cynthia.

"You said doctor's appointment. Everything okay with you?"

"Brian, do you really want to start learning about certain women's needs?"

"Uh, no, not yet," I said, and then giving her a quick peck on the cheek, I thanked her again for watching after Janey and returned to my car.

On the quick ride back to the farmhouse Janey kept stealing looks into the empty backseat. Puzzlement covered her face.

"You were gone a long time, Brian—where are the packages?"

"In the trunk, silly," I said. "I see I'm going to have to find a good hiding place, so you don't accidentally on purpose uncover them before Christmas."

"Brian, you can't do something accidentally on purpose."

"Oh, I think you could," I said, which made her giggle.

I left the packages in the trunk and joined Janey inside. It was already past nine, so I told her to get ready for bed. A few minutes later I went upstairs, found her already tucked in bed and reading a book to her frog. I sat on the bed's edge, smoothing her hair out of her eyes.

"How can you read with your hair covering your eyes?"

"It's not a very good book," she said.

"So why not read something else?"

"Because, Brian, I started this book and I have to finish it. Because that's what you do, you finish what you started."

It was good advice.

"Well, don't read too long, tomorrow's a school day."

As I readied to leave a few minutes later, Janey said, "I know where you can hide my gifts."

"Where is that?"

"Inside the windmill. That's what Momma used to do, every year. She would tell me the windmill was off-limits from Thanksgiving to Christmas. 'You never know what kind of project I'm working on, Janey.' That's what she would tell me. I remember, because even if I sledded down the hill and got too close to the windmill she would remind me of our deal. So go ahead if you want, Brian, it's another tradition."

"It certainly is, thanks, Janey."

I kissed her good night, shut off the light, and then wandered downstairs. As I fixed myself a cup of tea, I thought of Janey's suggestion. Wondered if it was less a suggestion and more a passive-aggressive command on her part. Whichever, I decided that's what I would do. I checked on Janey, who was sound asleep, and then, feeling like I could spare a quick fifteen minutes, I snuck outside into the cold night, gathered up the three large packages, and carried them from the driveway and through the field to the windmill. The sails were silent on this calm evening. I opened the door and set the bags down on the ground floor. Should I just leave them here in the corner, or was there a better hiding place? Then I remembered the closet upstairs in Annie's old art studio. So I wound my way up the circular staircase, the bags bulky in my arms. But eventually I stuffed them into the closet, closing the door with just enough room to spare. Then I impulsively sat down on Annie's stool.

Not much had changed inside the studio. Annie's easel was still set up, though no canvas adorned it. Her paints were laid out, though capped. Dried brushes occupied a jelly jar on the shelf. Surrounded by these tools that had revealed the inner workings of Annie's heart, I was suddenly enveloped by her presence. This room was special, as it was the first place Annie and I had made love, where we had poured out our troubles, where we had bonded over mutual sorrow, mutual betrayal, and later, mutual healing. In this room we had tried to forge a future.

Common sense told me I should return to the farmhouse, but I was caught up in the moment, allowing Annie's spirit to seep beneath my skin. I didn't want to let go; so little time had passed since she'd left us, but in other ways it had seemed an eternity. Being responsible for Janey, it was by far the most demanding role of my life, and also the most rewarding. I had wished for Annie and me and Janey to be one and instead

I'd had to settle for the knowledge that not all wishes are granted. My desires, though, meant nothing. Everything was about Janey.

Wiping away a tear that had crept out of my eye, I stood from Annie's stool, walked to the cabinet where she had stored her paintings. She had loved to paint the windmill over and over again, and had even given me one of them. As I flipped through several of the canvases, I smiled at the memory of first seeing these wonderful landscapes. How shy Annie had been, how modest she'd been of her talent. Before I realized it, I had settled onto the floor and was going through each of the drawers, coming upon many paintings, sketches, and pencil drawings that I had never seen before. I had never felt the need or the desire to intrude upon her secrets, sensing that I was going where I wasn't welcome. These represented Annie's past, her life before I had accidentally (on purpose?) stumbled into it. One painting in particular caused my heart to skip a beat, and that tear that I had wiped away earlier returned, this time bringing others with it.

In the bottom drawer I'd found a family portrait, Annie and her husband, Dan, and in the middle of them was an infant Janey, probably no more than three months old. Just like the photographs I had discovered in the attic last week, here now was further proof of the daunting task before me. Janey had once belonged to a loving family, a whole family, and circumstances, maybe destiny, had taken that from her, leaving her alone in the world, except for me. Was I constantly to be haunted by these memories, by all that Janey had lost? The past was a place you couldn't avoid, the littlest reminiscence able to spark them into the present. Like a painting, a ceramic windmill, even a shiny glass ornament. How was I supposed to respond to these memories? Try and hide them from her as a way of protecting her? Or was I just protecting myself, avoiding the pain? My own history claimed me as an expert at avoiding issues.

That's what I did, at least for now. I returned the portrait to the drawer, closed it to my eyes, though not my mind. Then I closed off the windmill, too, locking the door behind me as I retreated back up the snowy hill. Once I returned to the farmhouse, a surprising sight awaited me. Janey was sitting at the bottom of the stairs, clutching at her stuffed purple frog.

"Hey, Janey, what's wrong?"

"You weren't here."

"Oh, honey, I'm sorry," I said, immediately going to her side. "I went to put away the gifts and wasn't planning on being gone long. I guess time got away from me. But, Janey, you were sound asleep—and you never wake up once that happens."

She nodded her head slowly. "I know, but, well, I felt bad, Brian, that's why I couldn't sleep. I keep telling you these things, you know, ways Momma and I celebrated Christmas. But maybe you have your own ways of doing things. You don't have to hide the gifts in the windmill, and you don't have to chop down a tree for me, it's okay. I'll be fine."

"No, no, Janey, that's the last thing I want. I want to do what makes you happy. I enjoy learning about your Christmas traditions," I said, my mind blown by what she'd revealed. Here I had let slip my responsibilities by getting lost in the past, leaving her alone, and she was apologizing to me. I hugged her tight, trying to figure out a way I could take back my mistake. And then an idea came to me. "I'll tell you what, Janey, if it will make you feel better, how about I show you some of my holiday traditions?"

Her eyes brightened. "Like what?"

"Well, remember that big tree in New York we just saw being lit on the television?"

"Yes?"

"How would you like to see it for real?"

"That big tree, really?"

"It's where I used to live—New York City. I saw it every year when I lived there," I said. "So what do you say?"

She didn't answer immediately, but then said, "Can we go ice-skating?"

"Janey Sullivan, we can do anything you want to do," I said, silently adding that I would do anything for her. No matter what.

CHAPTER 12

"Janey, come on, we've got to get going," I said, running up the stairs to her room. I had my coat on, and my car keys were dangling from my fingers. Our latest adventure was upon us, and where was Janey? Not in her room, it appeared.

Maybe she was playing a game of hide-and-seek with me? I checked her closet, but came up only with a big mess of clothes and toys. I'd been lax about keeping her room clean, but maybe I'd been too easygoing. When we came back, she had some work ahead of her. I called out her name again, and again I got back nothing but silence. Not even one of her famous giggles. So, she wasn't playing, was she?

Still, I crouched down, my knees cracking. I didn't find Janey, but what I did discover took me by absolute, stunning surprise. I peeked beneath the bed, and tucked behind the rear front post was a familiar-looking box. It was obscured by some other stray clothes and toys. This messy room was very unlike Janey. Perhaps she was using all these items to try and hide the box? It was supposed to have been stored in the attic, and it had gone mysteriously missing. Well, no more. I'd found the little box that contained my family Christmas ornament. All this time wondering what had happened to it, and here it was stashed under Janey's bed. What was it doing here? Why would she do such a ridiculous thing as to take the ornament and then not tell me where it was? A wave of fear washed over me as I reached under the bed for the box. The sound of footsteps caused me to pull back, and I returned to my feet just as Janey entered her room.

"Hey, where were you?" I asked.

"In the attic. Sorry, were you calling to me? Guess I got lost in time, just like you did that other night when you were at the windmill."

"Yes, and what did we learn about that night?"

"Don't go wandering off—either of us."

"Right."

"Sorry," she said. But then her enthusiasm returned, a smile brightening her face. "But I was getting so excited thinking about seeing that big Christmas tree in New York, and that's when I started to feel bad because you never found that pretty ornament with your name on it. So I wanted to surprise you by finding it! I looked and looked, all around those boxes—Momma sure liked to keep everything, didn't she?"

I nodded, unable to use my voice for a moment. Finally, I said, suspicion in my voice, "And what did you find, Janey?"

"Nothing. Well, not the ornament. Sorry, we'll have to keep looking."

"Yes, we will," was my only reply.

She didn't react to that. She just said, "Okay, can we go, Brian? I'm really excited about the trip. Is your friend John as silly as you are?"

"We'll have to see about that," I said, not feeling very silly at all at the moment.

"I bet he is. I never knew grown-ups could be silly. Not until I met you."

But there was nothing silly about this moment.

I was sorely tempted to reach under the bed and retrieve the box. Confront her. But I couldn't do it, not now. We had too much ahead of us, today and throughout this holiday season. There would be a time for explanations later. At least I knew where the ornament was. I took cold comfort in such knowledge.

"Let's get out of here, we have a big day ahead of us," I said, and led her from her room. Neither of us looked back, and before long we were buckled into our seats and on the road. Again, we passed by the windmill, today looking lonely against a gray sky backdrop. As though it felt my mood. Even the sails were quiet. It took all my concentration to follow the road as we wound our way out of Linden Corners and back into the big, bad world. Our Philadelphia trip had gone well enough, but this new venture was something different. I was taking Janey to my previous life, the one I'd left behind on such an impulsive whim. Yes, it was time for sharing some of my traditions with Janey. But among them was the very obvious fact that I had a tendency to run from my problems. I eventually faced them, however, and now again I had another dilemma before me—what to do about Janey and the ornament.

She seemed oblivious to my frown. She happily gave a running commentary on all she saw out the window, other cars and piles of snow and in one case, a deer standing on the edge of the woods. Gradually the traffic increased as we got closer and closer to New York. It was a place I now associated with betrayal, and how appropriate was it that Janey accompany me back into this embrace. Seeing as how I had found proof that Janey had lied to me.

"You're very quiet, Brian," Janey suddenly said.

"Just nervous, I guess, about going home."

She frowned up at me, eyes dark. Then she settled into silence, staring out at the road.

CHAPTER 13

Thankfully those dark eyes didn't remain, as they were now as bright and alive as the sunshine that bathed the city. Janey's natural glow illuminated our day, shot off the glass buildings and reflective windows. And she accomplished such a goal with the utterance of one simple word.

"Wow."

These streets never fail to amaze and capture the imagination, and pictures can only show so much of its wonder. Nothing does its sights and attractions justice like actually seeing it up close and personal. This town was, of course, New York City, with its magnificent skyscrapers and bustling throngs of people, the pace of a place that barely stops to catch its breath. I'd been dazzled when I first laid my eyes on its urban sprawl, and now came Janey's turn. She was no less enraptured than I had been. I might have been keeping an eye on the road ahead of me, but for certain out of the corner of my other eye I stole a look at her face as the skyline came into view. Wonder gave way to awe, and for the present moment the problems that existed between us melted away, like hot water thrust on ice. Despite the anxiety I was feeling, there was no way I was going to ruin this trip for her.

"Wow," she repeated.

"Pretty neat, huh?" I asked.

"You lived here?" Her tone was one of incredulity, and actually at this moment I had to admit I felt similarly. Had I really called this steel and glass mountain home? I had, and for several years. Those years, though, seemed to have taken place so long ago, before the land of the windmill had swallowed me up and lifted me out of a stark reality and into its wind-fueled fantasy.

"Yeah, I guess I did."

I hadn't been back to Manhattan since August, since before the storm that had nearly destroyed the windmill and had changed us all, and the feeling that washed over me now was one of unfamiliarity. So much had changed. The place I'd once called home now looked as foreign as my parents' new home. As though both my childhood and recent adult lives had been wiped away.

We were driving along the FDR Highway, and at Ninety-sixth Street I took the exit ramp. Our first stop was on the Upper East Side, which I explained to Janey was where I used to live.

"That's where John lives now, right?" she asked.

"You got that right."

We had eventually done a lot of talking on the two-plus-hour trip down the thruway. I told her about John Oliver, how he became my best friend way back in our college days and still was my best friend to this day. He was my last remaining link to the city. I told her, too, how supportive John had been during my crisis earlier this year—the bout with hepatitis that had debilitated me and the changes that had occurred at the offices of the Beckford Group, my employer, both of which had precipitated my sudden and unexpected departure from the city. Last spring, life had seemed about as bleak as a Dickens novel, and just as lengthy, too. Distraction from wounded memories was exactly what I needed today, and no doubt John would provide that with his good humor and juvenile antics.

"You'll like him," I said. "But he's not as silly as me."

"No one is," she stated.

"Yeah? And you like me, right?"

"Momma always said, 'Don't say yeah.'"

"Oops," I replied.

Janey giggled. "See? Silly. No grown-up says 'oops.'"

As much as the mood had shifted on the ride down, she seemed dubious at the idea of liking this stranger who held the envious title of Brian's Best Friend. (My interpretation of how Janey saw certain things: Everything capitalized.)

So we parked my battered car on Eighty-third Street, just down the block from the brick apartment building I'd once called home. It was Sunday afternoon, and there were plenty of spots

available on the block. Some lucky Manhattan-
ite would score tonight when I'd vacate the spot.
For now, it was ours. I locked the car, grabbed
hold of Janey's hand, and the two of us made
our way down the quiet street.

"What are those black things on all the buildings—with the ladders?" she asked.

"Fire escapes."

"They look like ways robbers could break into
your apartment."

"Well, there aren't any robbers around, so
you don't have to worry."

We rang John's apartment bell, heard his voice
crackling through the intercom as he buzzed us
in. How many times had I taken these stairs, how
many times had I not even looked around—at
the scarred walls, at the dog hair that gathered
in clumps in the corner of the steps, at the
brightly painted front doors of each apartment?
Forest-green paint set against white walls. Nothing had changed, yet from my fresh perspective
as a newly christened "farmer," the boxlike living quality struck me as awfully confining. How
had I done it?

John was standing in the doorway, all six feet
two of him. He was dressed casually in jeans and
a sweater, not unlike Janey and me. All of us appeared ready for a day of adventure. I took care
of the introductions, with John bending down
so he was at eye level with Janey.

"Brian said you were cute," John said. "He
was so wrong."

Janey tossed me a skeptical glance. I gave him

a smiling look that said, "Go ahead, get out of this one."

But John, smoothie that he is, masterfully recovered. "Because you're far too grown-up to be called cute. That's for babies. You're very, very pretty, Janey. I like your freckles."

Janey blushed at John's compliment, and I laughed at his surprising level of charm. I edged past him with a knowing look, saying I wanted to see how he'd destroyed my place.

"Your place? I don't see any cows around here."

"Nice," I said, sarcasm apparent.

John's comment made Janey laugh, and suddenly it was like the two of them had been friends for years, poking fun at me their bond. John gave us the full tour—the bedroom, the kitchen, the living room, three rooms in one, with barely a decoration on the walls. His old place had been adorned with posters of rock groups and movies, but he seemed to be in a transitional stage. John Oliver, growing up? Who was this woman he'd fallen in love with? Did she have magical powers? One thing I did notice, set atop his dresser, was the postcard of the windmill I had sent him months ago. Nice to know there was a sentimental bone amidst his cynical nature. The tour took all of one minute, with Janey asking, "Where's the rest of the apartment?"

John assumed it was a rhetorical question. So he grabbed his coat and escorted us out of his building. As we walked to the corner to summon a cab, I whispered to him, inquiring after the "love of his life."

"Anna's meeting us at 30 Rock."

I took a step backward as my smile deflated. "Her name is Anna?"

"Yeah, why, what's the big deal?"

"Nothing, nothing, John, sorry, don't worry," I said, though a chill continued to run down my spine. Should I mention it? Had Janey even heard us? "It's just, well, for a second all I could think about was . . ." I indicated Janey.

"Oh shit . . . Oh, wait . . ."

"You said a bad word."

"Oops," John said.

Janey laughed, shaking her head. "Just like Brian."

"Sorry, Brian, you know, about . . . Annie."

"Guess the similarity in names took me by surprise."

"Man, it didn't even register, sorry," he said. "She going be okay with that?"

I looked back down at Janey, to find her looking squarely up at me.

"What are you two talking about way up there?"

"Grown-up talk," I said.

"Show me a grown-up," she said.

All of us laughed as a cab stopped at the corner of Eighty-third and Second Avenue. We hopped in, John telling the cabbie to get us to Rockefeller Center. Janey had been curious to ride in a cab, and now that we were inside one, she watched with caution as the driver began to weave his way through traffic.

"When do you pay?" Janey asked, leaning in close to me so the driver couldn't hear.

"When our trip is over."

She seemed to accept this, but still she kept glancing over at the meter as the fare clicked higher and higher.

Fifteen minutes went by as we weaved our way down Fifth Avenue. We got out at Fiftieth Street. Janey watched as John paid the driver, and before he could get his change a young couple was taking possession of our cab. "Thanks," they hurriedly said, practically closing the door on Janey's scarf. I pulled her out of the way quickly.

"You okay?"

"That wasn't very nice of them," Janey said.

"Welcome to New York," John offered.

The cab went dashing down the avenue, and we forget all about it. We quickly went in search of the tree at Rockefeller Center. Thing that size, it wasn't difficult to find.

There's no place like Manhattan for the holidays, Fifth Avenue in particular. The storefronts were extensively and, in some cases, excessively decorated, big red ribbons hung on the sides of buildings, a large wreath with gold and silver balls suspended over the intersection at Fifty-seventh Street and Fifth, its lights bright even in the blinding daylight. Janey guessed that it sparkled at night. At last we turned the corner and the tree came into full view. Standing nearly eighty feet into the air, covered with colorful lights, there was no denying its power, the hold it had over the assembled crowd of people. Probably thousands of visitors had chosen this moment to visit the tree, itself more than a tradition—this was an institution for the city of New York and a symbol for the season. Janey grabbed my hand and pulled me closer, to where we virtually stood beneath the great pine branches. She craned her neck, trying to look all the way up.

"Wow," she said with wide-eyed wonder, a word that would go overused this day. "It's so tall . . . but the buildings are even taller."

Her wandering gaze was interrupted when a new person joined our little group. Janey took a moment's break from the tree to meet John's girlfriend, who had just showed up.

"Wow," she said again, and this time, well, I have to admit I thought the same thing.

Her name was Anna Santorini, a nice Brooklyn-born Italian girl who was probably the very definition of beautiful. She was five foot six, had large brown eyes and short black hair that was flawlessly styled. It wasn't so cold that she wore a hat. Her lips were lightly coated with red lipstick. With her black coat and red scarf to match, colors that perfectly complemented her, she had caught more than our eyes. Envious men all over watched as John gave her a welcoming kiss on the lips.

Then he took care of the introductions.

"Wow," Janey repeated. "You're so beautiful."

"Thank you, Janey, what a very sweet thing to say. And quite the compliment, coming from such a beauty herself."

Well, that did it. Janey dropped my hand and took hold of Anna's, and for the rest of the day they would be inseparable. Not only did Anna provide a mother figure, but she was someone new to talk to. Not Cynthia, whom Janey had known for so many years; not good old, reliable Brian Duncan, who knew as much about little girls and what they really needed as he did about farming (despite John's humorous claims). In any case, the two ladies walked ahead of us while exploring Rockefeller Center, watching the ice-skaters below us, then across the street to the busy windows at Saks. Their new bond gave John and me a chance to reconnect. We talked non-sense, really, though I did concede my approval of the lovely Anna, whose personality matched her beauty. John positively beamed when I mentioned her, which made me wonder if Peter Pan had found an outbound flight from Neverland. I used to enjoy my visits to John's world.

Janey tugging at my sleeve stirred me from my reverie.

"Come on, Brian, let's go inside this store," she said, pointing to the entrance to Saks.

I laughed. "Aren't you a bit young for diamonds?"

"Yes, but I bet they have nice Christmas ornaments. Maybe you can get a new one, you know, in place of the one that's missing."

From this magical land I was transported back to reality, to the knowledge that Janey had taken the ornament and for whatever reason continued to lie about it. And here she was, suggesting we replace something that was irreplace-able. A shadow darkened my face as I realized I hadn't actually seen the actual ornament—just the box. Why was she so insistent that I get a new one? A horrible thought occurred to me, one I wanted to dismiss right there and then. No, there had to be some other rational explanation. She couldn't have broken my precious ornament.

"What ornament?" Anna asked.

"Oh, it's nothing," I said, wishing to downplay it.

But John, who had known me the longest, knew its significance. "The one from Philip?"

"Later, John," I said with pleading eyes. For once he actually listened to me.

We didn't go into Saks, and instead we resumed our walk down the crowded street. Gradually the terrible images that had flashed through my mind gave way to warmer memories of the life I'd had in New York. Even in this short amount of time, the city had changed, just as I had, just as Janey had. Lost in my world of Linden Corners, it was clear that the world that was New York still turned, life went on at its brisk pace, and I had to wonder if maybe I had missed it. Had my impulsive decision really turned out the right way?

CHAPTER 14

All four of us were headed for lunch at a Mexican place near Times Square. I directed everyone down Forty-seventh Street, wanting to at least walk by a store that held good memories for me. Eli's Jeweler's, the sign still read. I peeked inside the small shop, where I could see the little man busily attending to the wants of a happy couple. I smiled, glad that Eli was still in the business of selling dreams. As I was about to leave, Eli looked up and for the briefest of moments our eyes locked. I raised my index finger and spun it through the air, a handmade windmill. He nodded once in acknowledgment before returning to his customers and I returned to my friends. It was an innocent remark on Eli's behalf that had introduced me to the concept of tilting at windmills, though how prophetic his words had been only I knew.

We continued down Sixth Avenue, settling into the restaurant on West Forty-third Street. We placed our lunch orders. Janey announced to everyone, the waitress included, that all of the walking had made her very hungry. In time, chips and salsa, along with our drinks, were before us—wine for John and Anna, iced tea for me, hot cocoa for Janey.

"What, you're still not drinking? Thought the doc gave you the A-OK?" John said to me as I sipped my iced tea.

"Yeah, well, I've got responsibilities. Who needs it?"

"Brian, you own a bar."

"I run a bar. Very different from going to one."

"Semantics," he said.

I apologized to Anna. "Sorry, old news."

She informed me that John had given her a full debriefing of my new life and how it had come about. She asked about the windmill and what it looked like, and suddenly Janey jumped into the conversation, relating the story of how the Van Diver family had come to build the windmill out of necessity, how the Sullivan family had inherited the old farm and done their best to restore the great old mill to its former glory. I was surprised at the depth of knowledge Janey had, marveled, too, by her grand sense of storytelling. For an eight-year-old, there was lots of talent bursting out of those images. Who knew? Maybe we had a writer in our midst. Janey, though, was particularly modest when I complimented her skills.

"You really have to see the windmill your-self," she told them.

"Yes, I've only seen the postcard," Anna said.

"Oh, so you've been to John's place?" I inquired, half-mocking.

John shot me a look of surprise, but Anna just laughed it off. "Several times, Brian," she said, unapologetic.

"Wow, I never thought I'd see the day John Oliver was embarrassed about having a woman over to his place."

"Hey, Bri, there's a kid here," John stated.

That produced further laughter, even from Janey, who thankfully didn't understand why we were laughing but wanted in on all the fun. I was having a great time, and I was glad that Janey had been willing to make this trip. I loved my life in Linden Corners, don't get me wrong, but once in a while the open road called to me, that sense of wanderlust that had first captured my soul nearly a year ago. Or maybe my former life wanted me back, the city's raw energy calling to me. As much as Linden Corners was a morning kind of town, New York was quite the opposite, gaining strength with each passing hour of the day until the sun was down and the neon lights kept it awake all night. The switch in lifestyle had been a literal experiment in night and day for me.

Speaking of switches, the conversation took a major one. And not a good one.

"So Maddie left town," John informed with me with his customary lack of grace.

"Uh-huh," I said with more than a hint of indifference.

"Who's Maddie?" Janey asked.

There was silence at our little table for four.

"What, are we not allowed to talk about her?" John asked. "Come on, Brian, that's water over the bridge, I thought."

"Under the bridge," I said. "And I know all about Maddie. She's living in Seattle, she's happy, she's moved on with her life, and I'm glad for her. She's got a job with Microsoft and is making a mint. Just what she always wanted."

"That's not all she ever wanted."

"John, there's a reason why they call it the past."

"Okay, I'm sorry. I just wasn't sure, you know, if you were . . . over her."

"Who's Maddie?" Janey asked again. "And why do you need to be over her?"

Anna said, "She's just someone Brian used to know, it's not important now. Why don't you and I go pick out a couple of songs on the juke-box, Janey, what do you say? Maybe something with a good beat. Maybe we'll even get Brian dancing. Does your dad dance?"

Again, there was an awkward silence at the table—another sensitive topic broached, but there was no way Anna could have known that Janey never used the word *dad* when it came to me. Katrina Henderson and Thanksgiving all over again. But before I had a chance to explain, Janey simply said, "Not very well."

Then they went off to make their musical selections. Me, I selected John as my target and hit him on the arm, hard.

"I guess I deserve that—for bringing up Maddie," he said, his sorry way of apologizing. He'd always been sensitive to her side of what had happened. So she fell victim to corporate ambitions, he'd once said, it could happen to anyone. Anyone, that is, with the drive to get to the top and the willingness to sink to the bottom to get there. "You okay, though, you know, about that dad stuff?"

"Janey handled it very well. Better than I might have."

"I take it something like that's happened before? Can't be an easy thing to deal with, the poor kid. Makes me realize exactly what you've taken on with Janey. And don't get me wrong, Brian, Janey's great, and from what I can see, she's nuts about you. Is that enough, though, to get through, uh . . . this? I know it sucked what happened this fall. But you know, I keep thinking that maybe if you and Maddie had worked things out, maybe the two of you—and Janey? Hey, maybe it's not too late, since your old boss Justin Warfield and that dumb stunt from the spring are long gone. That's the thing about the past, you can leave it there, but people have to move forward, they need to make futures. Imagine it, Bri, you and Maddie and Janey?"

"I wouldn't do that to Annie's memory," I said rather forcefully. "Maddie is . . . Maddie's in a different time zone; hell, John, a different life zone. Let's leave it at that, okay? Enough couch-talk today. I'm fine, Janey's great, and we've got a great thing going. Let's talk about you instead—specifically, you and Anna. She's amazing."

"That she is, my friend, she's changed my life. Women, they can do that, in an instant."

Finally John was talking my language.

"Uh, can I ask you about something else?" John said.

"Something other than Maddie? I'd welcome it."

"You okay, you know, money-wise? And before you get yourself in a snit, I'm asking because I'm worried. Look at you, Brian. You're taking care of this little girl—and from what I can see, doing a great job. But that's a lot to take on; Janey's gonna need more than just your love; she's going to need security. And I mean financial security. Now, this is probably nothing that you haven't thought of, but, hey, can the two of you really survive on a bartender's salary? Especially considering you've had to hire part-time help so you can spend more time with her. You had your savings, but your six-month sabbatical from the world took care of a lot of that. So, I guess I'm asking, is everything being met? You know, end to end?"

As much as I didn't wish to discuss this with John, I knew he meant well. Just as he had when he mentioned Maddie. So I reassured him that everything was fine.

"At Thanksgiving, my father actually handed me a check for twenty-five thousand dollars. I endorse the check; he endorses my change in life plan. That ought to help for a while."

"Okay, good. I just wanted to make sure."

What I didn't tell John was that the check still was hidden away in a desk drawer. So much for endorsements.

As he took a sip of his wine, he assured me he'd covered all of the serious topics.

"At last," I remarked.

Our food arrived, and the four of us settled in for a grand old Mexican feast, quesadillas and burritos and rice with beans, the kind of meal that was scarce in the meat loaf and potatoes menu that Linden Corners subsisted on. Martha should have a fiesta day at the Five-O. There was lots more chatter, John and I dominating the conversation but only because we had so much history, so much to catch up on and to share with these new people in our lives.

Afterward, John insisted on grabbing the check, and I let him. We grabbed another cab that took us up to Central Park. From there, we ventured to the much larger Wollman Rink. The four of us rented skates and took to the ice. I had never been very agile when it came to skating, but Anna floated on the ice like a natural and Janey was a fast learner, and soon the two of them were whizzing by me and John, laughing and smiling the whole time, no doubt at our clumsy expense.

A while later, John and I gave up and we just hung out by the railing, talking. Though we talked often on the telephone, there was nothing like face-to-face contact, the conversation flowing much more naturally, the shifts from topic to topic less obvious. Luckily he said nothing more about Maddie. We talked mostly about holiday plans. John wasn't going home; instead he was headed to Anna's family for a traditional Italian Christmas Eve feast.

"What about you? You bringing Janey to your parents'?"

So I told him about my parents' plan to take a cruise. "New beginnings in the Duncan household."

"You okay with that?"

"I'm thirty-four, John, I've spent more Christmases than I ever thought I'd have with my parents. I think Philip would understand. Our tradition lives on, just in another form." He let the subject go, and then I told him about the annual party at the tavern.

"The social event of a Linden Corners Christmas," I said. "Why not stop by? See the cows for yourself."

"I hope that's not your way of referring to your clients . . ."

"Ha ha. I'm serious, come to the party."

"Brian, your little fantasy town is three hours away. Can hardly 'stop by.' "

"So, stay overnight at the farmhouse," I said. "You and Anna."

"You gonna wake me in the morning to milk the cows?"

"Hey, John?"

"Yeah?"

"You're such a jerk."

As the day wound down and night fell over the city, we walked back to the Upper East Side. It was not too far from the skating rink. The beautiful day we'd been blessed with had turned noticeably cooler, and I made sure Janey was bundled up. I was proud of her today, her resourcefulness, her willingness to try new things and to meet new people. And to walk, walk, walk. As worried as I had been about once again taking her from the known comforts of Linden Corners, I think with John and Anna we had given her an experience she wouldn't soon forget. They were warm and friendly and had taken to Janey like Santa takes to elves. The magical world that is Christmas in New York had gone perfectly.

CHAPTER 15

A dark night had fallen, stars sparse as clouds moved in over the region. We were exhausted from our full day's excursion that had seemed to take us through the busiest neighborhoods of Manhattan. It was in front of John's apartment building that we said our good-byes with hugs and handshakes, good wishes for a happy holiday. Then, as Janey and I made our way down the street, she turned back. Anna and John were locked in a tight embrace, kissing like teenagers. I watched Janey's wide-eyed expression, wondering just what she was thinking. When the two lovebirds finally broke apart, they saw Janey gazing up at them.

"You forget something?" John asked.

Janey shook her head. "I just wanted to remind you, you know, to come and see the windmill," she said. "You'd be very welcome."

We left them with big smiles on their faces,

hopped into the car, and sped away from the city. Traffic was light. The smile on my face didn't seem to want to dissipate either, not until a half hour into our trip, when Janey, who'd been quiet and obviously mulling over something in her complicated little brain, blurted out, "You never answered the question, Brian."

"Which one was that?"

"About the woman named Maddie. Was she your girlfriend when you lived here?"

"Yes, Janey, she was."

She was silent a moment, as though trying to absorb that information. Then she asked, "Were you going to marry her?"

"What makes you ask that?"

"Well, at Thanksgiving, your sister talked about that woman Lucy, and she said you wanted to marry her. And you told me that you were going to marry my momma. So, I just wondered . . . you know . . . about this Maddie woman." She hesitated, which was unlike her. Janey was the type to just attack a problem head-on, she tended to just blurt things out. And then she did, as she asked, "Did you also want to marry Maddie?"

I thought about Maddie, her platinum-blond hair, the way her voice would slip into its natural Southern tones whenever she got mad. I thought about that wonderful afternoon when we had strolled down Forty-seventh Street—the Diamond District—and how we had cooed together over a ring that absolutely sparkled in her crystal eyes. How the next day I had returned to purchase it, and how circumstances had brought me to return it without even having had the chance to present her with it. But on that return visit, good old Eli the Jeweler, he had had words of advice for me. All of us, he said, must tilt at windmills. And I had, literally and figuratively, as those words had taken me straight into Linden Corners, straight into the welcoming arms of Annie Sullivan, and the gently turning sails of the windmill. Had I wanted to marry Maddie? That had been my plan. But that had not been life's plan. And as much as I understood this, I reflected that Janey wouldn't understand the grays in life. Answers to her came in black and white, yes and no.

"I suppose, Janey," I said, "that yes, at one time in my life I did want to marry Maddie."

"Before you met Momma?"

"Yeah," I said, my voice barely above a whisper in the darkness of the car. Outside only the headlights guided our way home on the blackened roads. Janey didn't bother to correct my grammar this time. She merely quieted down again, her face scrunched up in thought. This adventure had yielded such deep discussions between us, and that was good because I wanted to encourage Janey to ask questions whenever she was curious. It was the only way for us to get to know each other fully, the way to keep the peace in the house. The reason for these trips, both to Philadelphia and to New York, was for Janey to get to know a bit about me, to know where I had come from and why being in her life meant so much to me. And maybe, if she began to feel closer to me, she wouldn't have pulled the stunt she had with the ornament. Perhaps we'd return to the farmhouse and she'd go running to her bedroom, take the box out from under her bed. Maybe a simple apology would come from her. Maybe it would suffice.

"Brian?"

"Yes, Janey?" I replied, concentrating on the road up ahead.

"You never told me about your family. I mean . . . your mom and your dad and Rebecca were at Thanksgiving, but why wasn't your brother, Philip, there? Why don't you call him? Maybe he can visit for the Corner Christmas party. You showed me his picture up on the wall, remember? I bet he's still so handsome."

I felt adrenaline rush through me and had my foot been more firmly on the accelerator we might have crashed into the car ahead of us. I eased back, took a deep breath. I felt a tear dampen my cheeks, emotion winning out over instinct. I pulled to the shoulder, flicked on my hazard lights. In the silence of the car, Janey looking up expectantly with her curious eyes, I turned to her, my voice a near-whisper, and I finally spoke the words I hated to say.

"Philip was sick, Janey, and . . . and he died."

INTERLUDE

That next night, as they slept peacefully within the warm comfort of the farmhouse, outside the wind had picked up, blowing wisps of snow across the open field, bringing to life the windmill's mighty sails. Gently they turned, then with more drive and energy and passion. And as those sails spun in the lonely night, a sound carried over the waves of the wind, a persistent whistle that awakened the little girl from her deep slumber. Though she didn't know what it was—who it was—she could undoubtedly feel a presence trying to reach out to her. She'd been dreaming of Christmas, of the gifts stored away inside the windmill until the morning of the twenty-fifth.

She threw back the warm blankets and dropped her bare feet to the floor. For a moment she listened for the sound of activity, and when she was satisfied that he was lost to sleep, she grabbed her robe and cinched it around her waist. She opened the door to her room, padded her way down the dark hallway. His own door was closed, but she knew he slept lightly, unlike herself, who enjoyed drifting deep down into the world of dreams. In fact, she couldn't be certain what had awakened her, if indeed she really was. Still, she felt the need pulling at her. So she ventured downstairs, where she put boots on her feet, a jacket over her robe, and thick mittens over her bare hands. A finishing touch of a wooly hat and she was ready for the outdoors. In the mirror that hung in the hallway, she saw her reflection and for a second she giggled; she looked ridiculous in this winterized pajama getup.

Once outside, she gazed high into the night sky. A brilliant half moon lit the sky, and little sparkles of stars lit her way. Through the snowy field she traveled, until she came upon the windmill's lone, majestic presence in the middle of the field. Backlit by the moon, it was like the sails were encased in their own glow, a sharp contrast to the black backdrop of night. She'd never before been outside at this hour and she knew it was wrong, but tonight that didn't matter. And even though she imagined she should be afraid, she didn't let her fear stop her. Of course, the door that led inside the windmill was locked, he had seen to it ever since deciding to hide the gifts here. Hadn't it been her idea? To see them, though, that wasn't the reason behind her nocturnal journey.

They had only been back from their New York adventure a night, and all day at school she had talked Ashley's ear off, describing the wonderful images of the holiday season she had witnessed. She also told her friend about Brian's other life—"He was smiling all day, Ashley, like he really missed his old home."

"Do you think he'll move back one day? With all his stupid things," her friend had countered with,

and that had set her busy mind reeling. What if Brian tired of her? Before going to bed that night, she had sent out a wish out upon the wind, hoping it would find her mother somewhere in her otherworldly travels. The wind always knew, because it traveled 'round the world and found every destination, even those hidden from the people who still lived.

Now Janey was certain that with the wind rattling against her window tonight, a reply had arrived.

She was feeling the cold penetrate through her outerwear, wanted to find a way inside the windmill to seek shelter. Then she remembered the spare key, and she reached down on the ground. A small crack in the structure had been the perfect hiding place for a key, and lucky for her, it remained there. Almost like it was meant to be. And so Janey unlocked the door and she made her way inside. But inside the windmill it was dark, and she had to wait a moment until her eyes fully adjusted to the lack of light. Then she circled her way up to the second level and emerged into her momma's studio. From there she peeked out the small window, realized her journey wasn't yet complete. From the second floor, another door opened to the catwalk that encircled the windmill. It was here Janey went, where she could see the sails pass right before her eyes, where she knew her momma had loved to watch the world go by.

She collected her thoughts before speaking. She thought about Brian, of the very first time she saw him right here, at the base of the windmill. Like he had appeared out of nowhere, and in her mind, that was fine. A virtual Brian Duncan was better than no Brian Duncan. But now, she was getting to know the

real person behind her magical version of Brian. She
realized there was a lot more to learn about him.

"I'm glad you called, Momma," Janey said, speaking into the wind. "Brian's been real good to me, just
like you said he would. He took me on a trip, actually
two of them, and I met all sorts of people he knows.
Momma? Did Brian really want to marry you? I
think so, because he's always wanting to get married.
There was Lucy and then some lady named Maddie.
Did you know about them? Brian says Maddie came
to the windmill once, but I don't really remember. I
don't want Brian to get married, because then I'll
have a new mom, even though Brian's not even my
real dad. People keep calling him that. I overheard
him talking with Cynthia—all he wants is for me to be
happy. He's worried about Christmas. Me, too, because I don't know what gift to get him. He has this
beautiful ornament that he's going to hang on the
tree. Except it's gone missing. Momma, can you help
me? That's all I ask. Because I thought I knew who
Brian was, and now, wow, there's so much more to
know. Momma, he has a sister who's not very nice
and he had a brother, but he died."

The wind blew past, the sails turned.

"Momma, I think I did something bad, and now
maybe Brian doesn't want to take care of me anymore.
He took me to New York and showed me places he used
to live and work and I met a friend of his. I had fun,
but I think Brian had more fun. He's been very quiet
since we got back from our trip. So that's why I think
he misses his old life. Do you think so, too? I'll wait to
hear from you."

So she watched the sails turn in anticipation of

some kind of response, not unlike the time before Thanksgiving when Brian had made his own visit to the windmill. If she listened hard enough, maybe an answer could be heard. Until then, she had to be contented with the chance to express herself.

"Thanks for listening, Momma. I love you and I miss you always."

She felt better just speaking the words. She felt warmer, too, even out in this bitter cold. As though her momma was feeding her strength, instilling within her an inner strength that could battle any temperature, weather any crisis.

"Oh, and merry Christmas, Momma."

Janey returned to the farmhouse, where she noted it was three forty-seven in the morning. Brian was still sleeping, and in seconds so would she be, clutching at her stuffed purple frog. A large smile would cover her face as she slept, peace settling over her. Maybe an idea was coming to her, too, on how to make Christmas special for Brian.

The next morning, she found Brian making breakfast in the kitchen.

"How did you sleep, sweetie?" he asked.

"Okay. I had a very weird dream."

Weird, because she had to wonder what her winter boots were doing beside her bed.

PART 2

NEW TRADITIONS

CHAPTER 16

While having noticeable drawbacks, living in denial was not without its appeal. I had not confronted Janey about the stolen ornament, feeling that once we opened that can of worms little good could come of it, upsetting the delicate balance we'd achieved. With all she had been through this year, with our relationship on unsteady ground and shifting daily, confronting her seemed the wrong approach. Also, I suppose I was waiting for her to broach the subject, and so far she hadn't seen fit to discuss the situation. And as the holiday neared, I allowed our busy lives to progress without interruption, telling myself it was just a silly ornament and her needs were most important, all the while ignoring the big issue. An issue of trust.

So instead, we turned a blind eye and concerned ourselves with other matters to fill our days and nights. In Linden Corners, there always seemed to be some event to look forward to. Since my arrival in town last spring, I had shared with the residents a joyous Memorial Day and been initiated into George Connors's summer tradition called First Friday. Myself, I had created a companion celebration at the tavern I had dubbed Second Saturday, in honor of kindly old George. Just this past fall I had rallied the villagers, who had come together to remember Annie in the most remarkable way possible, a true coming-together of community. So now it was with eagerness that I and my newfound friends in town were looking forward to the Christmas party at George's Tavern. We would hold it the night before Christmas Eve. I had been industrious in sending out personal invitations, and had also posted several flyers around town, at the bank and at the Five-O, as well as at the tavern itself.

As for Christmas, it was still more than a week away, though at the farmhouse it might as well have been two months off for all the decorations that adorned our home. Janey hadn't pressured me much either about a tree lately, and I guess I'd dropped the ball, so to speak. Of course, we hadn't been spending as much quality time together since the New York trip. She was filling her hours by playing with her friends and helping to plan her own school party. Cynthia had also called upon Janey for help with her annual tradition of bottling jars filled with jellies and jams. So, with the knowledge that Janey and I needed to solidify our holiday plans, it was with new resolve that I awoke that Saturday morning.

By day's end, I was determined that we would have a tree and our first holiday together would finally be under way.

At eight that morning I knocked on Janey's door, heard no reply, and when I opened it, she was already up. I made my way downstairs and found her in front of the television watching *Dora the Explorer* and laughing at the colorful antics.

"Morning," I said.

"Hi, Brian," she replied, not even looking away from the screen.

"You want breakfast? It's Saturday; what about pancakes?"

"I had cereal," she said, pointing to an empty bowl beside her.

"Oh, uh, okay."

I stood in the living room for a moment, feeling at a loss for words and hoping Janey might fill the void. She didn't, and eventually I went into the kitchen, made coffee, and pondered why I was being given the brush-off. Could she be reading between my words? Could she know what I knew about the ornament still under her bed? Now seemed like the wrong time to announce our plans for the day, which included chopping down our first Christmas tree. Deciding to tell her later, I showered and shaved and took care of some of the household duties I'd been neglecting. Some vacuuming, some much-needed laundry (not my favorite task), all of which kept me busy while Janey contented herself with an endless supply of cartoons. Around eleven o'clock, Janey popped her head into the laundry room and asked if I could give her a ride to Ashley's house.

"We're going to make cookies—Christmas cookies," she said. "Her parents promised we could."

"It's not on the calendar—when did you make these plans?"

"Oh, earlier."

"Earlier when?"

"What difference does it makes, Brian? I want to go to Ashley's—she's waiting for me."

"Well, she's going to have to wait longer. We've got plans today."

"We do?"

"We're going with Gerta to get the tree. We talked about this—earlier."

She didn't appreciate my throwing her own excuse back in her face. "Oh, well, you don't really need me for that. I'm too young to chop down a tree," she replied, then informed me that she was going to pack her bag, since she was probably staying overnight at Ashley's. She turned away from me then and I had to hold myself back from calling out to her. But I decided to let this incident pass—for the moment. Her attitude, her tone, had shocked me, and I needed time to absorb it, and to calm down. Had this exchange actually happened? It had been so un-Janey-like.

I let a long hour pass by. She didn't come to me again about a ride to her friend's. Perhaps she didn't really have plans, perhaps she had been testing me. Finally enough time had gone by, we needed to talk. Taking clean laundry to her room, I asked her to join me. With reluctance, she finally came up the stairs and sat on her bed, her arms crossed. She couldn't look at me.

"Janey?"

"What?" she said.

"I don't know what that was all about before, and I'm going to choose to ignore it. But what I'm not going to put up with is you not being there for the cutting down of the tree. You told me a couple of weeks ago that you wanted to get the tree, just like you and your momma did. It's a special memory, Janey, one I want to share with you. So I'll make you a deal, you join me and Gerta, then you can go to Ashley's later. But no sleepover, not tonight."

She said nothing. But in doing so, she spoke volumes. She wasn't happy being told what to do, and I wasn't happy having to be so firm with her. This was uncharted territory for us. Sure, she had been unusually distant with me a couple of weeks ago, but we'd weathered that after the day of sledding. Now, suddenly, since the trip to New York, the tension was back and stronger than before. Janey was learning the art of defiance.

"Come on, Janey, do we have a deal? I mean, imagine when Christmas comes and we don't have a tree decorated. I think that would make us both sad. Where will we put the presents?"

She gazed up at me, worry spreading across those cute freckly features of hers. For the briefest of moments, as no doubt visions of an empty Christmas morning filled her mind, I saw the Janey I knew, the Janey who had so completely stolen my heart. Who knows, maybe the day's adventure would cure her of whatever was bothering her.

She asked, hesitantly, "Can I pick out the tree?"

"Can you? Of course, you think you're just along for the ride? Your presence is vital. I've never done something like this before. You're the expert."

"Then okay," she said.

The barest hint of a smile had emerged, and I felt myself breathe easier.

Before I left the room, I kneeled down beside her and gently took hold of her small hands. She gazed right into my eyes. Her own were wet.

"You know, Janey, if something's bothering you, you can tell me about it," I said. "You can tell me absolutely anything. Okay?"

She nodded, but said nothing.

I kissed the top of her head and then went to call Gerta.

We had a tree to chop down.

CHAPTER 17

Green's Tree Farm was a good fifteen miles away from Linden Corners, just north up scenic Route 22. Janey and I had stopped first to pick up Gerta Connors. She was in need of a tree for the holidays, too, and I had agreed to help her chop it down. In the back of the truck I had packed an ax, as well as a saw. Ask me which was better for the upcoming task, I wouldn't know. Guess we'd find out. I'd never fetched my own Christmas tree before, not unless you counted going down to the local deli on any corner in Manhattan. Get your tree there for a hefty price, haul it home yourself. Took all of five minutes. So this adventure had all the hallmarks of something new and fresh and possibly laugh-inducing.

As we drove, Janey seemed to come around. As though the cloud she'd been living under had passed, the wind taking it and returning sunshine to her sweet face. Up in the sky, however, another weather pattern was brewing. Thick clouds hovered above us, and the snow had just begun to fall when we pulled into Green's parking lot.

"Glad I wore my warm boots," Gerta said, hopping into the cab of the truck. "Will you hold my arm, Janey, while we go hiking up that mountain?"

"Sure," Janey said.

"Thank you again, Brian, for helping me out."

"Isn't that what we do in Linden Corners?" I asked.

Gerta looked back at Janey, sitting in the rear seat. "He learned fast, didn't he?"

"Sometimes," Janey said.

They both laughed at my expense. I just drove, and finally we reached the lush forest. Snow-covered hills and endless rows of trees greeted us. We got out of the truck and immediately were taken in by the fresh pine scent wafting all around us. This was nature, and right now I was glad to be part of this trek into the wilderness.

Albert Green Sr., the rotund, jolly proprietor of the tree farm that had been in business for three decades, greeted us personally. He handed out a brochure that described the various types of trees we would find on our trek, as well as a map of the trails.

"Let me know which one you get, I'll give you top-notch instructions for caring for it," he said, his weathered face cracked with a smile. "Heck, you'll be able to keep it fresh till Memorial Day, ha ha."

"Why would we want to keep a tree in the house for that long?" Janey asked him.

We all laughed at her innocent comment, though based on her scrunched-up nose I could tell she'd been serious. Still, the happy exchange instilled in us the right mood in which to launch our journey. I figured it would be quick and easy, find a tree, cut it down, pack it up, leave. Not so when a fickle little girl is among your party, and she announces she's not leaving until she's found the perfect tree for Christmas. With thousands of trees surrounding us, I think Janey intended to inspect each and every one until she made a choice.

Green's Tree Farm was a magnificent spread, set against the rising thrust of the Berkshire Mountains. I realized we weren't far from the Massachusetts border, and who knows, the amount of time we spent walking through the cultivated, snowy paths, maybe we had already crossed into our neighboring state. Along the way we saw many other fellow tree-hunters, some of whom had been successful and were already carrying their prize trees down the side of the mountain and back to their cars. As I trudged through the snow, the cold winter air penetrated through my boots, and I felt envious of those who were headed back toward the warmth of their cars. But Janey's infectious joy kept me going, warming my insides. As she went running up the trails, pointing to tree after tree, then dismissing them with the grace of a queen before her subjects, she laughed and giggled and brought out smiles on my and Gerta's faces.

"Oh, that child," Gerta said. "So irrepressible."

No surprise, we found Gerta's tree first, since I think she was tiring of trekking through the snow and hills. We had to call to Janey, who was at least fifty feet ahead of us.

"Ooh, George would have loved this one," Gerta said, standing before an eight-foot, sweet-smelling Douglas fir. "He just adored the Christmas season. He was such a good man, but the reason he liked this season was, he said, it made other men good. Peace on earth, that was my George."

A picture of George Connors popped into my mind, him behind the bar and welcoming me inside its cedar walls, asking me what I'd like to drink. Recovering from a case of hepatitis, I had been forbidden to drink alcohol, and so I contented myself with an unexciting glass of seltzer. George had offered up no judgments, and it had been the start of a great, but far too short friendship between us. So now it was a distinct privilege to be chopping down his widow's holiday tree. Once again I felt like I was part of the Connors' family, not just their employee.

"Timber," I called out, feeling like a modern-day Paul Bunyan. Except I had used the saw, since I had no confidence in my ability with an ax. I might injure someone. That someone being me. As the saw slid out the other side of the trunk, the great tree crashed to the ground. From behind I heard someone say, "Yeah, but if we weren't here, would it still make a sound?"

We turned around to see Mark Ravens, my relief bartender, standing before us, an ax positioned ruggedly over his shoulder. At his side was Sara Joyner, wrapped up in a blue parka. Her face poked out from behind the fur lining, highlighted by her red lipstick. We laughed at his corny joke, shook hands all around. Janey had never met Mark before, and she smiled easily when he said it was nice to finally meet her. She, of course, giggled. He charmed her that quickly. They said they were there to get Sara's tree, since Mark was currently living with his parents and, as he explained, "They use an artificial tree. I hate those things, the pine scent is like one of those air fresheners used in cars. Helping Sara, well, that's been fun."

"He just likes using the ax," Sara said. "A macho thing, I guess."

I tried to hide the saw.

So Sara and Mark joined us in our search for the perfect tree, Janey explaining they could have the second most perfect. For the rest of our time, Janey kept soliciting Mark's opinion on trees, and when he declared one particular seven-footer to be "as perfect as perfect can be," our quest was finally over. I think Mark had sensed our weary nature. Gerta thanked him for his good taste, as well as his speed in finding it, and we laughed because we were all tired—except for Janey. Determined to put a crowning touch on the day, I asked Mark for his ax and after a couple of weak swings—and with the crowd cheering me on—I hacked my way through the trunk of the tree. As the thick wood separated itself from the base, it was Janey who this time yelled out, "Timber!" Sara chose the tree right next to the one Janey had picked and at last our day was complete, our mission a complete success.

We brought our three trees back down the mountain, loaded Gerta's and Janey's into the truck, and then paid Mr. Green. He said we'd picked some nice ones and did as he promised, gave us sensible instructions on how to keep them fresh throughout the season.

"And they'll look darned good with lots of tinsel," he told Janey.

"Icicles," she replied.

We said our good-byes to Mark and Sara, and as we pulled out of the lot, I caught sight of the happy young couple in my rearview mirror. They were locked in a tight embrace, kissing against the mountainous backdrop, snow falling all around them. As though they were part of a Hollywood movie, set designers working overtime for the perfect romantic moment. That was when I noticed Janey was watching them, too.

"Are they going to get married?" she asked.

"I don't know," I said, wondering what made her think such a thing.

"I think so," she announced with confidence.

CHAPTER 18

When we returned to the farmhouse, it was late afternoon and the sun had already dipped below the horizon. Cold air had settled over the land, so much so I could see my breath blowing before me. I asked Janey if she still wanted me to take her over to Ashley's. She declined.

"I don't need to see her, not today."

"What about the sleepover?"

"Nah, I didn't really want to."

"Okay, go upstairs and warm up. I'll take care of the tree."

She bounded into the house, leaving me to my happy work. I unloaded the tree and proceeded to unwrap the strings from its body. As I carried it into the backyard to settle back into its proper shape, the fresh scent filled me with the Christmas spirit. Suddenly I couldn't wait to decorate it, Janey and I singing carols while we adorned the tree with lights and ornaments and shiny tinsel . . . icicles.

I went inside and made some hot chocolate and took it up to Janey's room. She wouldn't be drinking the cocoa, not now. Guess the excitement of the day, or maybe the range of emotions that had toyed with her, had caught up to her. Whatever the reason, she was plain tuckered out and had fallen asleep. I tossed a blanket over her and closed her bedroom door.

When I returned downstairs, a knock came at the front door. I peered through the curtain, saw that Mark Ravens had dropped by.

"Hey, Mark," I said, while standing on the porch in my stocking feet. The temperature had dropped significantly in the hour since coming home. I rubbed my arms. "Quickly, come in. It's bitter out there."

"Thanks, hope I'm not disturbing you. I know you've got to get to get to the tavern soon. I've got work, too, down in Hudson. Got to hit the road soon," he said, removing his winter coat.

Saturday night was one of my nights at the tavern, and it was usually one of the busiest. But I still had a half hour before happy hour began. Besides, if I was a few minutes late, it meant Janey could rest that much longer. She was having dinner with Gerta and would then help her with her tree decorating. As they had said, the two were going to establish a new tradition. As it was, Saturday night was Gerta's regular night for watching Janey. I'd only asked Janey if she wanted to go to Ashley's to test her mood.

"So, what's up?" I asked Mark as the two of us

sat around the kitchen table. I grabbed two
Cokes from the fridge and set them down.

"It's about Sara."

"I figured," I said. "You two have gotten, what
should I say, cozier, since the last time I saw you?"

He smiled wide, the smile of a man in love.
"Oh, way beyond that, man. Brian, I'm crazy
about her. I think she feels the same about me.
It's funny, all those times I went to the Five-O, it
just never occurred to me to ask her out. I don't
why, maybe my hungry stomach ruled my blind
eyes when I was there. And then one day she's at
the tavern and I can't take my eyes off of her."

"Martha's waitress uniforms are not exactly
complementary."

He laughed. "Well, what I was wondering, since
things are getting serious, and I want to show her
that I'm responsible and all that. . . ."

"Mark, just spit it out. Work awaits us both."

"Right. Yeah. So, you know that apartment
above the bar?"

"I know it very well, as a matter of fact," I said.
"I lived there when I first moved to Linden Corners. Great little place. What, are you interested
in renting it?"

"Definitely. I've been saving up a lot of cash
living with my folks, and also what with the holidays here the tips have been good lately—at the
bar and down at the hotel in Hudson. So I'm
thinking maybe I can make a go of it, especially
if, well, if I ask Sara if she wants to live there with
me."

I was struck suddenly by Janey's earlier comment, wondering if these two lovebirds did in-

deed have marriage in their future. Moving in together was just the first step. If so, I had to give Janey credit for being the astute observer. I was happy for them, and proceeded to fill in Mark about the apartment's amenities and charms and drawbacks and suggested one night soon I give him the grand tour, "just so it's the right fit for you. And for Sara."

"Good idea," he said, "though I'm sure it'll be fine. What's the rent?"

"That's up to Gerta, Mark. I'm just the hired help. Gerta owns the building."

"Okay, I'll talk to her about it, thanks, Brian. I can't tell you what a big help you've been to me. A few months ago, I had no girlfriend and not much money and suddenly I'm in love and looking for a new place to live and thinking about the future. Man, who would have thought it, huh? Life can change on a dime, can't it?"

"Sometimes on a nickel," I remarked, knowing all too well what he meant.

I was glad to be able to help him get on his feet. Linden Corners had embraced me with such ease and genuine warmth, it was nice to return the favor, even if Mark wasn't exactly new to town like I'd been.

"Well, duty calls," Mark said, rising from his seat. "Thanks."

"Anytime, Mark. Let me know if Gerta quotes you a stiff price. I'll talk her down a few hundred."

Mark's face temporarily paled, until he realized I'd been kidding.

"I can't spend all my money on rent," he said.

"There's Christmas coming, and things can be expensive, if you know what I mean."

"Sure, sure," I said, walking him to the door.

He headed out, a noticeable spring in his step. As Mark's car pulled out of the driveway, I wandered into the dark living room and took a seat in the recliner. Using what little light was left of the day, I gazed about the room looking for the ideal spot for the tree. But as much as I tried to think about the upcoming holiday, I kept returning to Mark's cryptic comment. *Things* were expensive. Was he planning on buying a ring for Sara?

Life was moving forward for so many of us. For Mark and Sara, for my friend John and his girlfriend, Anna. I had to wonder, though, was it moving in the right direction for me, as well, and for Janey? Never in our short-lived relationship had problems existed between us. She was as charmed by me as I was by her. It had been like that from the moment we had met at the base of the windmill. She'd been playing a game that day. This morning, though, I'd seen another side of her and it had been no game. I had to hope that I'd seen the last of that behavior. I hoped the little bundle of energy who had taken forever to pick out the perfect Christmas tree remained.

Like I said, denial has its comforts.

CHAPTER 19

The joyous celebration was perfect, yet something continued to nag at me, distracting me. All night long I couldn't help but feel that I was missing something. Traditions old and new had come vibrantly alive, coexisting in a happy circumstance of togetherness. Laughter and stories of holidays past kept us entertained while trinkets glittered all around us.

It was three nights later, when, as a cold, blowing snow blanketed Linden Corners in acres of white powder and blustery drifts, inside the warm safety of the farmhouse, our winter wonderland presented itself as a rainbow of bright colors. The living room was in total disarray. Pine needles doubled as a second carpet and several boxes that had been brought down from the attic were strewn about, half-empty now after nearly two hours of decorating work. The result, though, was a mostly trimmed, beautiful Christmas tree. The string of lights circled the branches, the golden garland glistened against the array of red and blue and green and gold lights, ornaments adorned virtually every green branch. What remained was the crowning touch—our oft-debated subject of tinsel versus icicles. In the end, we had ceded each other our own traditions on this one, and so as Janey exclaimed, clapping her tiny hands, our tree would be extra special because it had both tinsel and icicles.

"Double the amount, lots of it to sparkle against the lights," she said.

Of course I had bought an extra box, so Janey could go at the decorating to her heart's content. Actually, she was very nimble with the thin strands, placing them with obvious intent upon the branches. Me, I had this habit of just tossing them, and when that went against the grain of her concentrated look, she pushed me aside.

"I'll do it, and I'll make it all nice."

I was spared any more tinsel-related torture as the telephone rang. I left her to answer the phone in the kitchen. Might as well make some hot chocolate and hot tea while I was at it.

"Hello," I spoke into the receiver.

"Brian, it's your father."

"Oh, hi, Dad," I said. The caller ID had indicated a "Private Number." Had I guessed who might have been calling, I would have been wrong no matter the number of chances given. I guess my voice betrayed me. "What a surprise to hear from you."

"Yes, Brian, I admit, it's rare for me to pick up a telephone—unless I need to check on my portfolio, you know." His comment, I assumed, required no response, and I waited for the reason for the call. "As you know, your mother and I are soon to leave for our cruise with the Hendersons. We're flying to Florida first, to spend a couple of days there before boarding. I was taking care of end-of-the-year finances, going over my accounts, and I was surprised to learn that you hadn't yet cashed the check I gave you. So I wanted to know if everything was all right."

How stupid of me to think he wouldn't notice. Dad watched his bank account like Santa checked his list. "No problem, sorry, Dad. I just haven't gotten around to it, uh, yet."

"Brian, might I remind you that it's careless to leave a check for such a sum of money lying around the house. You could lose it, it could get misplaced." He paused to clear his throat. I could visualize a quick sip of his Manhattan, helping to coat his throat. "Also, my accountant prefers that I not have all that money floating around out there in some financial netherworld. Especially at this time of year."

"Dad, tell your accountant that what you gave me is not a tax write-off," I said.

My father would not be deterred, not when it came to money. He was moving full steam ahead, no doubt his words scripted in his head. "Brian, giving you the check was not meant to hurt your pride, I hope you realize that. Like it or not, it's our way of helping you out. Cash the check, have a good Christmas with your sweet Janey. I'm sure the rest will come in handy in the new year as you figure out your financial plan. That's it, Brian, no more lecturing."

"I appreciate your concern, Dad, and I promise I'll head over to the bank tomorrow," I said. "Oh, before you hang up, did you and Mom get the invite? I was hoping, well, you know, maybe you could make it up to Linden Corners before the holiday. The cruise doesn't leave until the twenty-fourth, right? So you could make it. I want you to see where I live, where I work, meet my friends. Maybe have some of my own family around."

"It's a very kind invitation, Brian, but at this time of year it's just not doable. Your mother is helping with several charity functions, and I've got work piled up—if she and I are going to get away with the Hendersons, we'll need every moment until then. We leave on the twenty-second. Like I said, a few days of rest in Florida before we hit the high seas. I'm sorry, son."

"That's okay," I said, not surprised by their decision but disappointed nonetheless.

"Good-bye, Brian. And don't forget, first thing tomorrow . . ."

"I know, I know, go to the bank. 'Bye, Dad. Give my love to Mom."

"The same to you and Janey. Merry Christmas."

I hung up the phone and realized the teakettle was whistling. I turned it off without pouring the water into the mugs I'd prepared. Instead I returned to the messy living room, where I found Janey sitting on the sofa, strands of tinsel dangling from her fingertips.

"Hey, no breaks. Get to work," I said, jokingly cracking the whip.

"I'm tired," she said. "Can I clean up all this tomorrow?"

"Tomorrow? We're almost done. We're going to turn on the tree and sit and just stare at our handiwork," I said, sudden anxiety welling up inside me. First Dad and his typical distance, now Janey and her ever-changing moods. I didn't like dealing with either. Just minutes ago we had been having a grand time, and now she had grown sullen, not even looking my way as she addressed me. I'd only been gone from the decorating, what, ten minutes at the most? And hadn't she sent me off anyway? What could possibly have occurred during the time of the phone call and now had me coming up empty. I tried to coax her into finishing the tree, enticing her with promises of an ice cream sundae—"chocolate syrup and everything"—on top of the hot cocoa, but she turned me down flat.

"Good night, Brian."

I wished her pleasant dreams as she padded her way up the stairs. She disappeared at the top of the steps, the door to her room closing the only sound she made. I heard it rattle through the quiet of the night. I didn't hear another peep out of her the rest of the night. Had I blown it again? The interruption of my father's phone call had only been for a few minutes, but perhaps in Janey's mind it had been longer. Leaving her alone with the tree, no Dan, no Annie, and now no Brian.

Frustrated and guilt-ridden by these sudden

shifts in her mood, I busied myself by cleaning up the mess we had made. And when I finished, I turned off the lamp and sat and stared at the sparkling Christmas tree. Thoughts churned in my head, about Janey and about my parents, too, my mind ultimately settling on the issue of what to do with that twenty-five-thousand-dollar check. It was like it was toying with me, part of me knowing how sensible it was to deposit it, the other part feeling like I'd be failing Janey, and thus myself, if I did. Yes, I was loath to accept it, but my father had left me with little choice. He didn't make phone calls because he enjoyed them.

Maybe it was the phone call from my father that made me remember, but I realized the tree wasn't yet complete, at least not for me. What I'd been missing that night was my personal link to my Christmas past—the glass ornament with my name written in glitter still lay beneath Janey's bed, snug against the bedpost in its protective box, and I suppose I was still waiting for her to finally return it. Tonight it had momentarily slipped my mind, but now I knew that my mind had shut it out for now. Keeping the peace was important on this special night, one we would remember for years, our first tree trimming. I'd hoped having the tree up would inspire her to come around and present it to me; perhaps when she'd gone upstairs I'd considered she might be going to retrieve it. No matter how she returned it, it didn't matter. She could just say she found it, she didn't even have to accept responsibility for having had it all this time. I wouldn't be mad at her. Still, there was nothing from her camp on the issue, and she was already asleep. And beneath her sleep hid my family tradition. She continued to act as though she didn't know where it was.

As I sat back down upon the sofa and looked at the near-finished tree, I had to wonder if my parents, even with their pending trip, were putting up a tree in their new home. I doubted it, which made me wonder. Would they dust off their name ornaments and hang them elsewhere, perhaps over their hearth? And what about Rebecca, did she even care? Did a trinket from Christmas long ago really matter anymore?

Did anyone still remember Philip?

My first Linden Corners Christmas was quickly going downhill, on a sled suddenly out of control.

CHAPTER 20

The next morning, Janey came downstairs already dressed for school. I had breakfast ready, so the two of us sat down at the table, silence hovering between us. She had a healthy appetite this morning and ate her pancakes with gusto. She didn't comment on the fact that I'd deviated from our schedule. I usually only made pancakes on the weekend. I was still worried about her and me, and so I ate very little. Before she left that morning, she stole a look at the tree. The lights were off, and I thought it looked lonely.

"Wow, Brian, it's really beautiful, we did a good job."

"You haven't seen it with the lights on yet," I said.

"I'll see it tonight," she informed me. She gave it one last, studied look. "I bet the tinsel makes the shiny ornaments sparkle."

"Not all of them, the tree's not finished."

Even as I said it, I cursed my passive-aggressive approach. Thing was, Janey bit.

"Oh, right, your ornament. I feel bad, Brian."

"Why is that, sweetie?"

"Because you can't find your special orna-ment," she said matter-of-factly. "Oh, well, the bus will be here in moments, I better get down the driveway. We have a lot of snow today."

It was almost as if Janey was living in that same state of denial, as well. She just wouldn't confess that she'd taken the ornament.

After she left, I considered going up to her room and retrieving the box from underneath her bed and just placing the ornament on the tree. Then I could gauge Janey's reaction, but how would I explain it, that I was searching her room? That I was cleaning and found it? Even that sounded hollow. No easy solution pre-sented itself to me, so I busied myself with other matters.

I had the entire day to myself, and would use it to run some needed errands. Around ten that morning, breakfast dishes cleaned up, I trekked through the snowy field on a direct course for the windmill. Now that the farmhouse was deco-rated for the season, there was nothing left to do. Even the shopping for gifts was mostly done. As I made my way down the hill, the sight of the windmill made me take a step back, like always. The sails were quiet, barely moving on this espe-cially calm day. The winter storm from last night had blown by. A rich blue hue coated the sky, and the air contained a crispness that chilled my bones. I could easily see my breath in front of me. But what struck me most was that, in this season of gleaming lights and abundant joy, the windmill looked lonely and forgotten, its wooden carcass somehow colorless. It occurred to me to wonder if Annie had decorated the windmill during the holiday season. If she did, had it been for her and Janey's pleasure or for the enjoyment of passing motorists who could see the great old mill from the road? Blinking lights of blue and green and red and yellow struck me as the wrong chord. But maybe something more sedate, with more sparkle, like a night sky filled with stars. And, as though the windmill had inspired me, like always, I found myself liking more and more the pictures my mind had conjured.

To turn my new dream to reality, there was an errand I needed to run. I had to go to town anyway: A trip to the bank nagged at me. It had kept me up half the night. I had tossed and turned about what to do and ultimately realized my father would not leave it alone. So, to the bank I would go. Then I could stop by Chuck Ackroyd's Hardware Emporium, as well, to get the necessary supplies that would make the windmill sparkle in the night. Newly energized, I returned to the farmhouse, grabbed from the desk drawer the check my father had given me, and hopped into the car. Snow crunched beneath my tires as I made my way down the driveway and onto the plowed road. I found myself humming Christmas songs the entire trip into town, the holiday spirit reawakened within me. My fingers tingled against the steering wheel, and I contemplated the plan unfolding in my mind. Ha, take that, Martha—my windmill would outdo her old diner. As I parked the car and headed up the sidewalk to the Columbia County Savings Bank, I nearly collided with Cynthia Knight.

"Hey, Brian, look out," she called out, a bit too loudly considering I was right in front of her. She skirted around me with sudden flexibility.

"Oh, hey, Cyn, sorry. Guess I'm a little distracted."

"A little?"

I smiled. "Sorry, are you okay?"

"I'll be okay," she said, hand on her heart, her breathing heavy. "Just took me by surprise."

"And I've got my head in the clouds, dreaming up some last-minute details," I said. "Really, Cyn, if there's anything you need, you'd tell me, right? It goes both ways, us helping each other."

"I'd tell you if I could," she said enigmatically. "So you said something about a last-minute plan? Care to fill me in?"

"I'd tell you if I could," I said with a smile.

Calm now after our near-collision, she gave me a studied, curious expression. "Touché, Brian Duncan Just Passing Through. Guess it's a holiday filled with surprises. But still, color me intrigued about yours. You look like a devil with a plan on your pitchfork. While you're plotting whatever, can you melt some of this snow?"

"Nah, even I want a white Christmas."

"Well, in any case, I'm glad I ran into you. I've got some last-minute shopping to do at the mall and I was planning to go tomorrow afternoon. Bradley needs some new shirts for the office and he hates department stores, so I thought I'd wrap up a few for under the tree. Men are so difficult to buy for. Bradley needs a distraction from work, work, work. Tell me, would you like that, new dress shirts?"

"I don't wear dress shirts anymore, so no, I wouldn't like them."

"Gee, so helpful you are," she said. "Anyway, I was thinking maybe Janey would want to join me. I hate shopping alone and the idea of having a little girl with me . . . well, what's better at Christmastime? Do you think she'll hate the idea?"

I laughed. "Hate going to the mall? Janey'll love it."

"Perfect, I'm excited. Besides, the holiday is fast approaching, and I figured she needed to do some shopping of her own," Cynthia said, sporting a knowing look. My guess was, this impromptu trip to the mall had already been discussed and needed only my approval. "Also, there's that gift drive that St. Matthew's is having, part of their annual toy drive. You know, donate a gift for the less fortunate. I need a kid's opinion on what another kid would like."

"Good idea," I said. "Thanks, Cyn, Janey will have a ball."

She returned to her car, walking gingerly on the icy sidewalks, and I realized I had lost an opportunity to ask if Cynthia had detected a change in Janey's behavior. Or was it reserved only for me? I could have solicited her opinion on what might be bothering Janey, but in the end I was glad I hadn't. Cynthia had taken on enough responsibility in helping out with Janey; the last thing she needed was to hear my whining. She was our friend, not Janey's mother. This problem between me and Janey, it was mine to figure out. Janey and I would make it through, I told myself, though the conviction was not as strong as I might have wished it to be.

Pushing those thoughts to the back of my mind, I went inside the bank and filled out a deposit slip and then handed it and the endorsed check to the teller. The teller raised her eyes at the amount, but said nothing to me. He just took care of the paperwork.

"Will there be anything else, Mr. Duncan?"

"As a matter of fact," I said, sudden inspiration hitting me, "there is. Do you know when this check will clear?"

A few minutes later I left the bank, the distaste in my mouth I entered with no longer present. Leaving my car at the bank, I headed for the hardware store down the street. Linden Corners's business district was that easily negotiated.

Ackroyd's Hardware Emporium was owned by the surly Chuck Ackroyd, a longtime resident of Linden Corners and not my biggest fan, even though we had seen each other through the fiercest of storms last summer. It had been a rare meeting of our minds that hadn't been repeated to this day. Chuck had been one of George's regulars, one of his good friends, too, and resentment had reared its ugly head once George embraced me as he did upon my arrival in town. Jealousy is a useless emotion, but some choose to find strange comfort in it. As I walked into Chuck's busy store that day, the bells jangling above my head, I saw him standing at the information desk. I nodded hello, and he pretended to occupy himself with something other than saying hello back. Not even the holiday season could help him, though in fairness to him, he had no one close with whom to share it. His wife had run out on him years ago, and he hadn't fully swallowed that bitter pill.

Guiding a cart with wobbly wheels, I ventured down a crowded aisle still overflowing with Christmas accoutrements and decorations, lights and power strips and angels to put atop a tree, finally picking out several boxes of white lights. Then I went in search of extension cords and more staples for the staple gun I'd used to put up the lights at the tavern. When I had all I required, I made my way to the cashier and paid for them. Chuck came by to bag my purchases, casting me a wide eye as he stuffed the numerous lights into the brown paper bag.

"You lighting up the sky with these?" he asked.

"No, just the windmill."

He harrumphed. "You and that windmill. I don't get it."

"Merry Christmas to you, too, Chuck," I replied, wishing I hadn't allowed him to goad me. I turned back to him with a fresh smile and said, "So, see you at the party this weekend?"

He shrugged. "Probably not."

I was about to brush him off, but that's what he expected me to do. Imbued with the holiday spirit, I took another tactic. "We would like you to be there. Your invitation was sent by me, yes, but it really comes from Gerta. She still considers you a dear friend of the family—you were there for her during the funeral and after and are still. This year's party is another passage for her, Chuck, the first holiday without George. Don't disappoint her, Chuck. Besides, you never know who'll show up, maybe make you smile."

"I'll think about it, Brian," he said.

Wow, he actually said my name without a sneer. Well, there was progress for you.

I had one more errand to run, and so I returned to the bank's parking lot and got behind the wheel of the car again. I pulled out into light Linden Corners traffic, a phrase most might call oxymoronic, and made my way around the corner to St. Matthew's Church. Aside from our occasional Sunday excursion to mass, the memory that stuck with me was this past summer when, during that fierce storm, many of the residents sought refuge within its sturdy walls and basement. Unfortunately, much of the beautiful stained glass that covered the windows was blown out by the howling wind, and it was still being repaired. No simple task, not only because of the artistry involved, but the financial concerns, as well.

I rang the bell of the rectory, and almost at once it was answered by none other than Father Burton himself. His smiling, aged face looked at me with surprise, but still he welcomed me in like a sheep returning to its flock.

"Brian Duncan, why, it's not Sunday," he said, amusement written across his face.

"No, that it's not, Father. I wonder, do you have a moment?"

"For Linden Corners's favorite son, of course I do."

"I'm hardly that," I said.

"Son, since you've come to our fair village, you've made more than an impression."

"Thank you, that means a lot."

He ushered me into his small office. A pencil-sketch rendition of St. Matthew's had been hung over his desk, along with the obligatory cross. For a man who had spent most of his adult life at this parish, his office was surprisingly impersonal, in direct contrast to the warmth I discovered in his face.

"So, what can I do for you?"

"I suppose I've come for advice—about Janey."

"A charmer, that one," Father Burton said.

"She's presented me with quite the dilemma this Christmas, and I'm just not sure how to handle it," I said, and before I even realized it I launched into my story of the missing ornament. He listened with intent, nodding but not interrupting. When I finished, he stood up and asked that I follow him. We left the rectory, crossing into the church itself. All was quiet, our feet echoing against the hard floor. I allowed my eyes to wander, gazing at the stained-glass windows, at the way the light pierced their color and bathed the church in a warm glow. I could well imagine Father Burton enjoying his solitary time inside this sacred church; it held a power much like the windmill. It inspired, it taught, just by being. Man's creation brought to life by the faith it drew in us all.

Yet even the most beautiful thing can be damaged, and in front of a boarded-up, broken window was where Father Burton stopped. It had been damaged by this summer's fierce storm, a tree branch crashing through it. Months later, the window remained unrepaired; stained glass was a concentrated art, and it would take a while before St. Matthew's was whole again.

"Do you remember which of our panes was damaged?" he asked me.

"I'm not sure I understand."

"What did the stained glass illustrate?"

I think I knew what he was getting at. It was all too appropriate. "The Madonna and child," I said.

He nodded knowingly. "Brian, life hands us many challenges, and it's how we react to them that makes us stronger . . . or not. Janey Sullivan is a damaged girl right now, no matter how happily she laughs, no matter how much joy she brings you. To handle all she's had to endure, she's done remarkably well. I credit your guidance. Many adults couldn't handle it, and many men would not have taken on such responsibility. She lost her mother, and right now . . . you, Brian, are that glue. You are what is holding her together. Until she's ready to heal, she remains a fragile being. She may not even be able to control her emotions. If, indeed, she took your ornament, she may not even understand her actions. But to confront her, it would sound accusatory." He paused. "Children are like glass, Brian."

I found myself looking at the remaining windows, thirteen stained-glass representations of God, of faith, of the enduring human spirit. They were whole, complete, but any moment that could all change.

"Thank you, Father Burton," I said. "You're very wise."

We shook hands, and with my heart heavy, I made my way out of St. Matthew's. Errands complete, I was actually looking forward to getting home.

When I returned to the farmhouse, Father Burton's words continued to reverberate in my mind, and I was hopeful to share his earnest wisdom, if indirectly, with Janey. First, though, I went about emptying my trunk. I hid the lights I'd purchased inside the windmill's closet right alongside Janey's presents, not ready to put into action my plan for them. It was a big project, one that required an early start.

By the time Janey came home from school a couple hours later, with a frowning Ashley in tow, I had completed all my errands and was sitting quietly, doing research on the computer. I wouldn't mind one more errand, however, the idea of driving Ashley home not without appeal. Janey hadn't asked in advance if her friend could come over, but I chose to say nothing as she happily showed off the Christmas tree, informing her friend that she had hung most of the ornaments herself, even the higher ones. She didn't share the fact that I had lifted her up to assist in such a task. It was almost like I hadn't been there to decorate the tree at all. Of course, nothing was said about the one ornament that was missing from our tree.

"Brian was busy while I hung all the ornaments," she said suddenly. "He was busy talking with his father on the phone." She made sure that I overheard her. The exaggerated comment, combined with the icy tone in her voice, penetrated my skin and wounded my heart. I left them to play, not wanting to hear anything further. When Ashley's mother came to pick her up, Ashley stuck her tongue out at me. Why didn't I like this child?

Dinner passed without incident, and later, when Janey was getting ready for bed I sat on the edge of the bed as I usually did.

"You had a good day?" I asked her.

"Oh yes. I like when Ashley comes over to play, she's fun to be with," she said. "And I'm sorry I forgot to tell you she was coming. That wasn't very nice of me."

I nodded. "Just remember that for the next time."

"I will, I promise," she said, and her voice was so filled with sadness I felt a need to cheer her up.

So I told her then about Cynthia's idea of the two of them taking a trip to the mall tomorrow afternoon. Excitement returned to her as she had something to look forward to the next day. Kids, they operated on such a short schedule.

Tomorrow was important, but the months and years ahead, they could wait.

"And who knows," I said, "maybe there'll be a surprise waiting for you when you return."

Her eyes lit up. "Can you give me a hint?"

"As a matter of fact . . ." I paused before saying, "No."

"Hey, you faked me out!" she said.

"Consider my surprise something special to dream about," I said, and then kissed her on the top of her head. As I was leaving her room, I turned back, saw the whites of her eyes staring up at me through the darkness.

"What is it, Janey?" I asked, wondering if this would be the moment of truth for us. She'd already apologized for her thoughtless behavior of bringing Ashley over without asking beforehand. So I had to hope that confession would open the floodgates for more truths.

She hesitated and in the end just shook her head. "Nothing."

"You sure?" I asked.

"Yes, Brian. But thanks, I know you're always there for me."

Despite the conflict that ran through me, I let it go. Let her sleep, we'd talk tomorrow. "Okay. Good night, Janey Sullivan. I love you."

"Good night, Brian Duncan. I love you more."

CHAPTER 21

Janey had been given her instructions: go directly to Cynthia's after school, do not pass "Go," do not collect two hundred dollars, do not unwrap any presents, and most certainly, do not come to the farmhouse, "because I won't be there when you get home from school." So I said. That was a necessary little white lie, because the notion of putting up lights all around the windmill was daunting at best and I needed the time to get it done right. No peanut gallery making comments like I'd had to endure from Martha. Decorating the tavern had taken an entire morning, and that wasn't nearly the number of lights I was planning to use for this project. I had a lot of hanging, a lot of stapling ahead of me. Fortunately, the weather chose to cooperate, and the arctic air that had earlier settled over the region these past few days dissipated. Temperatures hung in the high thirties.

Melting snow created a bit of slush. Still not ideal, but better than twenty with a wind chill in the teens.

I had set up all the necessary tools down at the windmill. Two ladders, the staple gun, the lights and extension cords I had bought, as well as a thermos of hot coffee to keep me warm while I toiled all day outside. So at nine o'clock I began to work, and as the clock ticked, the staple gun clicked, and I strung strings of lights all over the great windmill—on the tower, the cap, the tiny windows. What continued to puzzle me was how to get lights on the sails. It was too impossible a task, I considered, since their constant rotation would just get the wires all tangled. It was a logistical problem that continued to elude me as the day progressed, and as lunchtime approached, I was still left without a solution. I took a break and returned to the farmhouse.

I wasn't in the kitchen two minutes before I saw Gerta's car pull up in the driveway. She stepped out, carrying in her hands one of her famous strawberry pies.

"Well, this is a pleasant surprise," I said, opening the front door to admit her. I tried to take the pie from her hands, but she said she could manage.

"Oh, I've made several more for the party, but I knew to save one for you, dear," she explained, setting it on the kitchen counter before offering up a kiss to my cheek. "My goodness, Brian, you're frozen solid. What have you been doing, sleeping on ice?"

"Hardly. But I have been outside most of the day. You know, you're not the only one with a surprise up their sleeve. For now, though, it remains a secret," I said. "If you want to come back later today—after sundown—you can see for yourself what I've been doing."

"Very intriguing, Brian. But very well, I'll let you get on with your surprise. I've got some shopping to do."

"Got time for lunch first?"

"Are you cooking?" she asked warily.

"I'm getting better at that domestic stuff. Can't exactly order from the corner deli and expect it to be delivered in fifteen minutes. Linden Corners is very definitely not New York. I was only going to make a sandwich. How badly could I mess that up?"

"I suppose I'm about to find out," she said, taking off her coat and placing it on the back of the chair.

So Gerta joined me for a quick meal of ham and cheese sandwiches, pickles and chips and a cup of tea. She continued to prod me into confessing what I'd been working on. I continued to say nothing, letting my grin toy with her. Eventually she changed the subject.

"Oh, Brian, that reminds me, I meant to talk to you about a matter that has come up. That nice boy Mark Ravens came to see me, asking about the apartment above the bar. Asked me what the rent was. I told him to talk to you about all the details, but he said you had referred him to me. Goodness, what do I know about things such as rent and maintenance? Are utilities included, or are they extra? George handled that kind of stuff. And since you were the previous tenant, I would think you'd have a better sense of how much you paid, certainly more than me. I told Mark I'd get back to him. But really, Brian, I've given you free rein over the tavern. All those decisions are yours."

"I know, I know, but Gerta, that bar is your family's legacy. I'm just the caretaker. You're the caregiver."

"I have four daughters, none of whom make Linden Corners their home. What interest do they have in running a bar? Hmm, seems I'm going to have a make a decision after all."

As we finished our sandwiches, I suggested dessert.

"I know you, Brian Duncan, you're just looking for an excuse to cut into that pie. Don't let me stop you." She paused and allowed herself a happy smile. "You better cut two pieces."

Gerta left shortly afterward, and I returned to the windmill with a full belly and a contented feeling. I spent the next three hours putting up the last of the lights, finishing with the railing that encircled the second-level catwalk of the windmill. At last, I was out of lights and had made all the necessary electrical connections. I ran the extension cords inside and plugged them in; thankfully the windmill had working outlets, and I only hoped whatever circuit breaker they were on could handle the amount of power required.

When I had put away all the tools in the barn,

I returned to the windmill and ventured upstairs to Annie's studio. I gazed about, sensing her presence inside.

"Well, Annie, I don't know what kind of traditions you and Janey had when it came to the windmill, but, well, here's a new one, I hope. New traditions are good, they give you a sense that, even though it's the first time, there is intent for something longer, something everlasting. I only wish I could have found a way to light up the sails. How beautiful they would have looked turning against the dark sky."

It was good that I had finished my lengthy task. Darkness was settling upon the region. I returned to the farmhouse to wait out Janey's return, and at six thirty I heard tires crunching against the driveway. I went out to meet Cynthia and Janey, and like clockwork, behind them in pulled Gerta. She had run into them at the mall, conveniently enough.

"Sorry we're late. Janey wanted to watch the little kids visit Santa," Cynthia said.

"And then Gerta walked right past us. What a surprise to see her there," Janey said.

"Well, I'm glad you're all here. I have something to show you."

"So you've said. I told Cynthia and Janey, and we all hightailed it over here. So, Windmill Man," Gerta said, "what's the surprise?"

"Follow me," I said.

And they did, the four of us trekking through the snowy field and down the hill, the moon guiding us on this black night. Cynthia asked for Janey's hand, and together the two of them trailed after me and Gerta. They almost looked like mother and daughter, bundled up against the falling temperatures. Winter had officially arrived today, and snow was once again in the forecast.

"Okay, stay there. I'll be right back," I said to the three ladies in my life, feeling like a kid at Christmas who couldn't wait for someone to open a gift I'd given them. Because I knew how special it was and I wanted to share it with them.

I dashed inside the windmill. The surge protector was turned off, but the extension cords were already plugged in. All it took was one flick of the switch, and I readied my finger, praying that this went off in real life as successfully as it had in my mind. Why hadn't I attempted a trial run? Because I didn't want to see it by myself—it was a thing to share. So I hoped that all went as planned. Then I quickly depressed the red button and even though I was inside the darkened windmill, suddenly I was cast in a warm, glowing bath of light. From outside I heard loud exclamations, like a crowd reacting to a spectacular fireworks display. I ran back out and rejoined them, all of us staring upward. The windmill was lit up like a giant spinning angel, set deep against the heavens.

"Oh, Brian . . ."

"Wow . . ."

"Sweet Lord . . ."

So said Cynthia, Janey, and Gerta, respectively. As they reacted just the way I had anticipated, clapping, talking, pointing, I studied my daylong handiwork.

The windmill was ablaze with white light from top to bottom, hundreds of twinkling stars adorning its quiet façade, as though they had fallen from the sky to brighten our path on this darkest of nights. And even though the sails themselves had no lights upon them, what I'd inadvertently and unexpectedly created was a magical shadow effect, with the bright glare of the lights that covered the tower emitting strong, powerful beams that, set against the dark blanket of night, were thrust through the open slats of the sails. The wind picked up and the sails turned, and then the light flickered against the ground, shadows dancing amidst us. The effect was more than I could have wished for, and as the light reflected against our awed faces, I couldn't help but think of Annie Sullivan, of her special spirit and how it continued to inspire me and feed me enduring strength. As if sharing my thoughts about her momma, Janey came to my side and wrapped her arms around me. I held her tight, and for a moment the world consisted of only the two of us, Janey Sullivan and Brian Duncan, she who called this home, me who once was just passing through this magical town and now could also call it home, and in our eyes and our hearts was Annie, the woman who had singly, miraculously brought us together. Annie had blessed us today. It was the shortest day of the year, one I wished could have lasted forever.

CHAPTER 22

The magical night of the lighting of the windmill wasn't over, not yet. The four of us stood for who knew how long, marveling at the illuminating sight before us, basking in its glow before finally feeling the evening's bitter cold penetrate through the layers of clothing we wore. The wind had definitely picked up, and snowflakes had begun to drift down from the sky. I invited them all back to the farmhouse, where we made good use of the strawberry pie Gerta had brought over earlier. Gerta, though, was tired and so she left shortly afterward, saying she'd see us tomorrow at the tavern.

"Brian, she's so looking forward to the party— I think she had given up hope of having her annual celebration," Cynthia said. "Connors' Corner might have been George's domain the rest of the year, but on that particular night, Gerta ran the place with a smile as addictive as her pies. And she loved every minute of it."

"Well, I'll be behind the bar and so will Mark, who arranged to get the night off from his hotel job just so he could help out. Though I suspect he has ulterior motives." I paused, taking a sip from my mug of tea. "So, that will allow Gerta to play lady of the manor and welcome all our guests. It should be fun."

"What will?" Janey said, bringing in her empty pie plate from the living room.

"The big party tomorrow," I said. "You ready for it?"

"You bet."

"Good," I said. "So what do you say you get a good night's rest in preparation."

She rolled her eyes and said to Cynthia, "He's not very subtle."

"Ha ha, off to bed, Little Miss Big Words," I said, pretending to chase after her. She went running up the stairs, squealing with delight. I told her I'd be up in a minute, then asked if Cynthia minded staying for a while longer.

"I was planning to, if you don't mind—I need to talk to you about something."

Curious about what might be on her mind, I told her to hold that thought while I went to check on Janey. By the time I got upstairs Janey had already brushed her teeth and thrown her pajamas on and was settled under the covers with her book. We talked for just a couple of minutes, because even though her pleas of wanting to stay awake said otherwise, her yawns betrayed her. As I got up from the bed, she said, "Thanks, Brian, for making the windmill sparkle. Momma would have loved it."

"I'm sure she can see it."

"It's so bright, I bet they can see it on all the other planets," she said.

I flicked off the light, and with a full heart, returned to the kitchen. Cynthia was pouring herself a fresh mug of tea.

"I'll take a refill," I said.

We sat down at the table, both of us ready to dig in to the topic we each wished to discuss. Which turned out to be the same.

"I want to talk about Janey," we both said, and then laughed.

"You first, Brian, what's going on?"

Despite my earlier reservations about involving Cynthia in Ornament-gate, I knew I needed some guidance. Janey and I were walking a slippery slope, and one misstep and we might never heal. So I filled in Cynthia about everything: the shifts in mood and the attitude, the brashness with which Janey wore her newfound, limited independence. "She's become unpredictable, Cyn. Some nights—like tonight—we're totally fine, and then others, yikes, she won't even listen to me. I hate to be firm with her . . . but I know I have to be. I'm her guardian. Who knows, maybe it's the stress of the holidays and this shall all pass after the New Year. Or maybe she misses Annie so much she's uncertain how to deal with her emotions. Whatever's truly bothering her, it's not good for her—not good for us. Janey and I are only going to work if we can keep open the lines of communication. And that's what she doesn't do, communicate. She shuts down."

"Have you said anything to her?" she asked.

I confessed that I tended to avoid confrontation, that was my style. "Always has been. Keeping the peace is my motto," I said, thinking of how quietly I'd left New York last spring. There had been no big blowups, no arguments. I'd become an emotional steel trap and no animal dared penetrate. Only life in Linden Corners had opened me up again, to heal and to feel.

"I sense there's more you're not telling me," Cynthia said.

"Wow, Cyn, you're good," I admitted. I told her then about the case of the missing Christmas ornament, it's having gone missing nearly the minute I'd brought it back to the farmhouse, discovering it under Janey's bed. I confessed my fears and my avoidance. What I didn't tell her was why it was so important to me. "I don't want to upset the delicate balance that already exists between us. And I know how silly this sounds, it's just a stupid tree ornament."

"No, Brian, it's anything but silly—or stupid. Obviously the ornament is important to you, otherwise you might have dealt with the issue already. Maybe you're not ready to speak of its significance, that's why you're letting it remain undetected under her bed. But you do need to clear this matter up—and fast. You can't have those suspicions hanging over you. It will damage this Christmas and maybe all the others, too. Get the ornament back, first of all. Go under the bed, get it, hang it on the tree. Then you need to talk to Janey about it. But I'll tell you, Brian, she's mentioned the ornament to me several times and all she's ever said was how pretty it is. I didn't sense that there was something wrong there," Cynthia said, allowing herself a pause. "As for the behavioral fluctuations, well, let me approach this from another angle and see if we can't find some common road. Today at the mall, it was all I could do to keep her focused on the gift buying. All she wanted to do was look at the people—mostly at couples. Holding hands or even kissing and she would make comments, like . . ."

"Like they were going to get married."

"She's done that with you, too?"

I related the story of seeing Mark and Sara at the tree farm, how our day had ended with Janey's question about their possible marriage. "It seemed to come out of left field, Cyn. But then Mark comes to me later that same day, asking to rent the apartment above the tavern. He's going to ask Sara to move in with him, and I wondered if maybe there was more to his actions. He practically admitted that he was getting ready to propose. How Janey guessed it, I don't know."

"Obviously, it's what's nagging at her mind, whether she realizes it or not. Her actions toward you—that brashness you spoke of—might not be so deliberate, Brian. Perhaps her subconscious is playing tricks with her, making her act out. Even she might not understand why she's saying what she is. She's acting on impulse, instinct. Not rationality."

"I'm hardly a trained psychologist—add in the complex workings of a child's mind and I think we'd have an easier time with a thousand-piece jigsaw puzzle of a blizzard."

She laughed. "I wish I had a perfect solution for you. But really, Brian, talk to her. You can't be afraid to. Remember, you're the grown-up."

"Sometimes Janey questions that, too," I said, a rueful smile crossing my lips.

"Like you said, a delicate balance. You have to be the disciplinarian, but you also want to be the fun guy she met from this summer. Not easy to be both. But I think so far you've managed beautifully."

"Thanks, Cyn, it helps just being able to talk about it. I'll watch her mood the next couple of days, and if her shifting moods persist—or worsen, God forbid—then I'll have to take some kind of action. Who knows, maybe if we talk about the ornament, everything else will fall into place. I'm sure it's all wrapped up under one big 'issue' somewhere in her mind. For now, I just want to get through Christmas."

"You know, that could be it, too, Brian. She did confess one thing to me."

"What's that?"

"She said, and I quote, 'For Christmas, I want to give Brian what he most wants.'"

"And did she offer up what that was?"

"Nope."

"Hmm, the plot thickens," I said.

Cynthia got up from her chair, putting empty tea mugs in the sink. For a moment she stood over the counter, her body wavering. It seemed almost like she was going to faint. Hastily I stood and went to her side.

"Hey, you okay?"

"Yeah, yeah, just a wave of . . . nothing. It's nothing, Brian."

"You know, you're acting kind of funny," I said.

"Just tired, Brian. The moment passed, I'm fine. Guess I better get home to Brad."

"You okay driving home?"

· "Brian, worry about Janey," she said, offering up her friendly smile. Color had returned to her cheeks, and she appeared steady on her feet again. So I allowed her to go, not without a hint of concern. She said she and Brad would see me tomorrow at the party.

After she left, I mused over our conversation. Standing over the sink full of dirty dishes, I realized my mind was full of unanswered, nagging questions. Dishes and questions could wait. I went upstairs to check on Janey, who was fast asleep. Her purple frog, though, had fallen to the floor and I bent down to retrieve it. After placing the frog back in her protective arms, I returned my attention back to underneath her bed. Tucked against the bedpost was the little brown cardboard box, still undisturbed from when I'd discovered it earlier. Hearing Cynthia's words in my head, I realized that she was right, I needed to just take back the ornament. There was no more delaying the issue; no more denials.

And so I withdrew the box from its hiding place, my hands shaking as I opened the lid. My

mouth dropped as I stared inside the box—the
empty box. The Christmas ornament wasn't inside it. My heart sank as I considered what I
should do next. Afraid now that Janey might
awaken and discover me hovering above her, I
returned the box to where I'd found it and
quickly left the room. I headed to my bedroom,
leaving the door slightly ajar, as I always did. But
I wanted to close it fully and hide from the
world. Indeed, the plot had thickened, and I
was now at a complete loss as to what to do.

When finally I slipped beneath the covers of
my own bed, I wondered if I could possibly have
dreamed up the discovery under her bed, and
knew that was just wishful thinking. Here was a
further complication I hadn't expected.

What had really happened to my ornament?

CHAPTER 23

The day of the annual George's Tavern Christmas party finally arrived, and there was so much preparation involved, Janey and I barely saw each other that morning. Considering my non-discovery under her bed, she and I needed to talk, that much was obvious. The timing had to be just right—no distractions. But there was no denying I was devastated by this latest turn of events, and as Mark and I went about our routine of checking the taps, dusting the bottles, and shining up the bar, I found myself walking around in a fog.

"Hey, Bri—you with us today?"

"Yeah," I answered, my voice on autopilot. "Why?"

"Well, for starters, you're polishing the plastic pitchers."

So I was. I put down both towel and pitcher

and suggested we take a break. "I could use one," I said.

"How 'bout you show me the apartment now?" Mark said.

"Great idea."

It was three in the afternoon, an hour away from the start of the party. Cynthia Knight had volunteered to help Gerta bring over the food, and her husband, Bradley, had gone to St. Matthew's to borrow a long table on which to set out the delicious buffet. So, with the bar mostly set for a night of revelers, I grabbed the keys out of the register and waved Mark onward.

"Keep in mind I haven't been upstairs in a while, so it might be a bit musty."

Mark didn't care, he was twenty-four and on the verge of getting his first apartment. The roaches could have given him a welcome parade and he'd have been thrilled, not that we had roaches here at the tavern. There were two ways to get to the upstairs, through a door that was located right behind the side of the bar, or through a separate back entrance. The apartment consisted of three rooms—a bedroom, a living room, and an eat-in kitchen, each room generous with its allotted space. A good-sized bathroom completed the layout. Furniture came with the place, I said as we headed up the stairs, "but, of course, if you want to replace it with some of your own, go ahead. I'll just store the stuff in my barn."

"Oh no, I don't have anything."

"Well, Sara might," I said pointedly.

He nodded eagerly. "Oh yeah, right. Not that I've said anything, not yet."

"Your secret is safe with me."

With a flourish, I threw open the door to the apartment and allowed Mark to step in first. He gazed around, his grin increasing the farther he ventured forward. He gave the place a good inspection, and as he did I allowed the memories of this past summer to wash over me. What a terrific place this apartment had been, just enough space so I hadn't felt cramped, but not too big that I got lost. My needs had been simple then, a perfect match for a home that needed only a willing tenant to infuse it with life. And judging from Mark's reaction, the apartment had found its newest occupant. I was glad to help him move forward with his life.

"How long did you live here?" he asked me.

"I don't know, let me see. Five months or so, until I moved into the farmhouse."

"Right. And what about all those nights you didn't work at the bar, was the noise level loud?"

"You can't hear a thing from downstairs. Good solid floors, along with the two doors at either end of the staircase, manage to keep out all sound from below. And I would assume vice versa. They don't build them as solid anymore."

Mark grinned. "I'll take it."

"We haven't talked about the monthly rate."

"I'll take it," he repeated.

And so he did, our hands shaking on it. We agreed to work out the particulars later, and I agreed to be fair with the rent. Then we returned

to the bar, where Gerta and Cynthia were already
busy bringing in dishes, and Bradley was noisily
setting up the metal folding table against the far
wall. I had at least proved my point, that you
couldn't hear a darn thing that went on below.

"Here, let me help," I said to Brad.

"Hey, stranger, good to see you," he said. Brad
Knight was my age, and I usually saw him dressed
in a suit, white shirt, and tie, the busy lawyer setting out for the office. Today he was dressed in
blue jeans and a holiday sweater.

"Yeah, I know, haven't seen much of you.
Seems every time I visit Cynthia you're still at
work."

"Billing a lot of hours this time of year," he
said. "Gotta save up."

"For what?" I asked.

"Wait till Christmas," Brad said.

Once the table was set up, he offered to go
get the chairs out of his trunk. He said no more
about what was going on with him and Cynthia.
I stole a look across the room, where a smiling,
rosy-cheeked Cynthia was lighting one of those
Sterno heaters. She didn't look any the worse
for wear, considering her near-fainting spell the
other night.

In any case, Christmas was just two days away,
so whatever news the Knights had could wait.
For now, Linden Corners was ready to celebrate
this most special holiday, where families joined
together for a joyous time and friends became
that much closer. George's Tavern, while a place
for adults for every other occasion, today was
open to the entire public. We were about com-

munity, not alcohol, though that wasn't to say we weren't serving to those of legal age. The food was on us, the drinks on whoever wanted one, that was the deal and we received nary a complaint as the tavern began to fill up. By six that evening it was wall to wall people, the jukebox was playing only Christmas-themed songs, people were engaged in games of pool or were talking at tables, against the wall, leaning against the bar. The mood was festive, and it had an infectious hold over me as I worked. I pulled the tap with a smile, filling and refilling glasses, just like George had taught me last summer. And Gerta, she stood over the trays of food—fried chicken and plates of lasagna, sausages and peppers and potatoes and vegetables, rice and shrimp, breads and rolls, and for dessert, pies, pies, pies. A veritable feast for a variety of folks.

My regulars had all turned out. Even Chuck Ackroyd showed up, busy now talking with Martha Martinson—who had closed the Five-O for the occasion. "Hey, I need a night off from cooking; but good thing Gerta only does this once a year, she's better at cooking than I am at telling jokes," which was quite an admission from her. A dreamy-eyed Sara Joyner was there, hanging out at the edge of the bar, talking with Mark whenever he got a free moment. Marla and Darla, who owned the shops down the street, could always be counted on for a party, and just as they had done last summer at First Friday, they sat there doing tequila shots and trying to outdo the other. Competition, thy name is twin. Brad and Cynthia were dancing to the Eurythmics' version of "Winter Wonderland," which had slowed the party's tone down some.

"Hey, we worked hard," Brad said, "so I've earned a slow dance with my wife."

The song ended and then the joint was rocking again, with Bruce Springsteen's "Santa Claus Is Coming to Town."

At six thirty, I was about to offer Mark a break when a surprise guest arrived through the front door and my mouth nearly dropped. It was my friend John Oliver, and at his side was his lovely girlfriend, Anna. I informed Mark that I was taking the break instead, and went over to greet my friend with a huge welcoming hug.

"Man, I can't believe you're here—you never confirmed with me, you know?"

"Where are the cows, Bri?"

Anna slapped his arm, saying, "You said no farm jokes."

"Oh, uh, then . . . surprise!" he said, holding up his hands.

We all laughed and then I escorted them over to the bar, where I asked the twins to give up their seats for a while. They grumbled at first, but when I gave them a complimentary shot, they acquiesced, jointly stumbling off to get some much-needed food. John was impressed with my managerial skills, less so with my bartending skills.

"Where are our freebies? We drove all this way."

So I poured John a draft and got Anna her requested glass of Chardonnay, warning her, "Wine's not our specialty," and then set about taking care of introductions. John met Gerta and Cynthia and Brad, even Chuck came over to say hello, more interested in Anna's form than in being friendly. "They sure got pretty women in that city," was his crass comment. I recalled he'd been equally taken with Maddie when she made a surprise, last-ditch visit last summer to repair whatever had once existed between us. Still, Chuck's behavior did little to dampen my enthusiasm. Having John and Anna here in Linden Corners was the perfect mingling of my old world and my new life.

"Where's Janey?" John asked.

"With her friend, Ashley," I said. "Her parents promised to come by for dinner around seven, let the kids dance and have fun for a couple of hours. Probably good that she's not here the entire time, I've been swamped since we opened the doors." I paused, then slapped my friend on the arm. "Hey, I'm glad you're here, John, it means the world to me."

"No problem," he said. "But I hope there are some accommodations in this rinky-dink town of yours. Saw some place called the Solemn Nights. Hope you got better."

"Stay at the farmhouse, no debate."

"Oh good, I get to wake up and milk the cows."

Both Anna and I ignored him.

With those details settled upon, John and Anna got some food and started to mingle with the kind townsfolk of Linden Corners, they easily welcoming them, especially after I announced, "These are my friends from the city and they want to go cow tipping later." That got a huge laugh and before long the city slickers were engulfed in a group of locals who began to debate the pluses and minuses of country life.

Janey showed up finally, with Ashley and her parents, Chris and Lea Baker, nice churchgoing folk who I don't think had ever stepped foot inside this bar; or any other, I thought. They had met at church, she taught Sunday school and he helped out with confirmation classes, or so they told me one day when I'd picked up Janey from their house. As they helped themselves to food, Ashley turned around and stuck out her tongue again. This time I fought back. I stuck my tongue out at her.

Janey, though, didn't notice our exchange. She was all smiles, especially when I scooped her up and brought her behind the bar. I let her use the soda gun to pour drinks for herself and Ashley, for Ashley's parents, too.

"Wow, Brian, I think everyone's here tonight. Wait . . . is that John? Hi, John! Anna!" she screamed out from the bar, waving wildly as she did so.

Janey got sucked into their world, and I could tell she was clearly delighted to see Anna again. Relief flooded over me as I realized the Janey we all knew and loved was here. Smiling, giggling, her infectious personality keeping the party mood high. She was a natural at working the crowd, charming them with her little laugh. As I watched from behind the bar, I at last offered Mark the break I'd promised him. He tossed his dirtied apron on the shelf under the bar, pulling out from a hidden spot behind some bottles a small vial of cologne. He splashed it on, then shrugged when he saw me watching.

"Hey, it was good enough for Sam Malone on *Cheers*," he remarked.

He disappeared into the sea of people to find Sara. When they embraced, her happy shriek rose above the noise from the jukebox.

As more people arrived, Gerta stepped in to help behind the bar, and with her at my side, time passed quickly, easily, and before long another hour had passed and Mark hadn't yet returned. Not that I minded: In truth he wasn't even scheduled to work tonight, and was doing this as a favor mostly (though he was working for tips, which tonight were very good). I was about to send out a search party for him when another surprise presented itself to me. My mouth hung open so widely, I might have been catching barflies.

"Rebecca?"

CHAPTER 24

"Rebecca?" I repeated, my eyes blinking but the image somehow remaining. I realized that was exactly the person who had just walked through the front entrance of George's Tavern. My unpredictable sister, wholly living up to her reputation right now, and behind her, equally surprising, was her son, Junior, a small, wiry kid with dark hair and glasses. Thrust into such unfamiliar surroundings, the din of the crowd and the music blaring, it was no surprise that he clung hard to his mother. I didn't remember him as the garrulous type. It must be hard to be with a mother as vocal as Rebecca.

Wearing a slinky dress and a wry smile, she made her way toward the bar. She caught the attention of more than one patron. I slipped out from behind the bar and grabbed her with more enthusiasm than I'd intended. As we pulled apart, I said, "You know, you look just like my sister."

She punched me.

"Same personality, too," I said. "Hi, Junior, how are you? Good to see you."

He looked up at his mother, unsure of me. I hadn't seen Junior in over a year; which meant he hadn't seen me, either, and so his welcome was anything but enthusiastic. But he did finally shake my hand with a surprisingly firm grip, and in return I tousled his hair, hoping to get a smile. He tried a tiny one before giving up. My sister and I hugged again, which was rare, as well. But I was overcome by the fact that they had showed up; I had considered my parents coming a long shot and Rebecca an even further one.

"We would have been here sooner, but I got lost. Thankfully my headlights caught sight of the windmill you always talk about—otherwise I might not have known we had found what we were looking for. I blinked, nearly missed it. It's a really small town, Brian." Then she gazed about the crowded room. "Not that you can tell with the number of people here. Let me guess, free booze?"

"Ha. Free food, yes. The booze you gotta pay for."

"Even for family?"

I mixed a cranberry and vodka for Rebecca, then a Coke for Junior, and when they were settled with some food I called Janey over. Surprise was written across her face when she saw Rebecca, but at least she remembered her and politely said hello. I introduced Janey to Junior, glad to finally do so after Rebecca had failed to bring him to Thanksgiving. Junior was ten

years old and just a couple of inches taller than
Janey. He was way more shy, too.

"I'm playing with my friend, Ashley, but you
can join us. Wanna pick out some songs on the
jukebox?"

"Can I, Mother?"

Rebecca gave him a dollar for the music, saying, "Have fun, Junior. Take good care of him,
won't you, Janey?"

The kids went running off, and after I served
a couple of patrons some refills, I returned to
my sister's side to sneak in a moment's conversation. Our parents had left for their cruise, her
ex-husband was off to see his own parents somewhere out west, leaving Rebecca and Junior
alone for the holidays. "So I figured, why not,
Janey and Junior would meet eventually, so why
not take care of it now? And I wanted to see
what this windmill thing was all about. Though
I'd like to see it up close in the daylight."

"You couldn't see it with all those lights on?"

She had no idea what I was talking about, and
then I realized that in my haste today to get
everything ready for the party I had forgotten to
flip the power switch. The windmill tonight
stood shadowy against a dark sky, alone. Linden
Corners was alive with the holiday spirit, but
Annie was darkened, quiet. I wanted to dash out
right now and light the windmill, but I had responsibilities here. So I assured Rebecca she
would see the windmill before night's end, "and
don't worry, it's quite a sight."

While we talked and she drank, I learned that

she had dumped that guy Rex soon after Thanksgiving. "We were never serious, I just brought him to piss Mother off. She hates the men I date; the ones I marry, too, which is not always mutually exclusive. It's nice to give her something to complain about. For us it's conversation. Ol' Rexy served his purpose—in many ways and many times." Ignoring her innuendo, I happily changed the topic. I insisted that she and Junior stay overnight at the farmhouse, thrilled at the idea of having a houseful of guests.

As I'd been talking with Rebecca, a flushed Mark Ravens returned to his post behind the bar, and a short while later Sara resurfaced. Her hair was slightly askew and I didn't have to venture a second guess about where they'd been and what they'd been doing all this time. Good solid walls, indeed. But Mark's return enabled me to take a break myself. I wandered outside to get away from the noise and the crowd and take in some fresh air. I left Rebecca talking with, of all people, Chuck Ackroyd, who wanted to know, "Is this pretty lady from the city, too?" I decided to leave the discoveries to themselves.

Snow was falling on this crystal night, cars and sidewalks lightly coated. Though I didn't have a coat on, after the heat of the bar I welcomed the bracing air. I stepped off the porch and wandered away from the building, glad to have a moment to myself. There was no denying that the annual tavern party was a smashing success, and apparently I'd done a good enough job of telling my friends and family how important it was to me. That John and Anna were here was remarkable; Rebecca bringing Junior so he could meet Janey, that was one for the ages.

I was feeling the chill now and remembered my coat was in my car, so I went to retrieve it. Voices coming from the back steps halted my progress. I recognized one of them as Janey's. I was about to make a hasty retreat when I heard the word *father*, which made me stop in my tracks. If I made a noise, I might be discovered, and that would be far worse than what I was really doing. Because I was curious to hear what she had to say, and while eavesdropping wasn't in my nature, given all that had been going on between me and Janey perhaps I might gain a little insight. So I listened in.

"He's not, you know, my father," Janey said.

"I didn't think so," said Junior, his squeaky voice distinctive. "I mean, I haven't seen Uncle Brian in, uh, well, at least a year and I didn't remember him having a kid then. Or even being married. He was always the guy we saw at Christmas, or sometimes visiting him in his tiny New York apartment. So you can't just show up one day with an . . . eight-year-old girl and say 'Look, I have a kid.'"

"Nope."

"So what happened?"

"My real father died many years ago. And my momma, a bad thing happened to her—not so long ago. It's probably not nice to say, but I miss her more. My father I know more through the stories Momma told me and the pictures she

showed me and just a few of my own memories
of him. But Momma? There are lots of memories there. What about you, you're lucky—you
have both a mom and a dad."

"Except they don't live together. It's because
they always fight, and sometimes those fights are
even about me," said Junior. "I think you're the
lucky one. I like Uncle Brian. He's . . ."

"Silly," Janey said.

"Yeah."

"But he's very good to me, Junior. He makes
me pancakes for breakfast whenever I want, and
he takes me on trips—I went to New York City
and saw the biggest Christmas tree ever—and
one day all we did all day was go sledding. He
even took a turn. It didn't go so well. Then he
made me the best hot chocolate."

"Sounds like a dad to me," Junior said.

"Except he's not." There was a moment's
pause and then I heard Janey say, "Do you think
it's possible someone can have a father and a
dad?"

"Maybe. I mean, my father will always be my
father, but sometimes when my mother gets a
new boyfriend she asks me whether I wouldn't
mind having a 'dad' around the house. That's
what she calls them. Luckily she's in between
'dads' right now, so it will be just her and me for
Christmas."

"Did you decorate a tree?"

"Yeah, even though we're not home to see it.
She insisted, 'cause we had to hang our special
decorations."

"An ornament with your name on it?" Janey asked.

My ears perked up, hoping for some new information.

"I got mine the year I was born—I'm supposed to think about my Uncle Philip when I hang the ornament, but I didn't even know him. So I just try and find a high branch and hope that I'm taller than the year before."

I had heard enough, and fearing that if I lingered any longer they would discover me, I crouched back to the front of the building as quietly as possible. Before returning to the bar I wiped my moist eyes, not from the cold. Tears had started to flow as I'd listened to them, these two complete strangers, bonding over the saddest idea imaginable, the notion of lost parents. I was grateful to Junior, who had miraculously gotten Janey talking, thinking maybe now that he'd opened the gates, the flood might pass through the village and find its way home. So Janey and I could heal whatever rift had come between us.

The rest of the night passed in a blur, so focused on Janey was I. The food was gone, the pies had been served, and the number of guests had begun to dwindle down to the regulars. Ashley and her parents were long gone, but Janey had opted to stay. She and Junior were quietly playing cards at a table in the far corner. When the clock struck eleven, I realized they were still wide awake and I suggested maybe it was time to get them back to the farmhouse.

They'd probably crash the moment we got back. I mentioned this to Mark, who offered to close up the bar.

"Maybe keep it open awhile, the tips are good."

"Keep in mind, only regulars remain."

"Oh, right, so much for tips."

"We heard that," said Marla and Darla.

"Okay, Brian, but before you go I have an announcement to make," he said, and then, because he wanted the remaining crowd to hear him, he climbed on top of the bar and whistled for everyone to quiet down. Someone pulled the plug on the jukebox and suddenly the bar was filled with rapt silence, everyone staring expectantly at Mark. I caught a glimpse of Sara out of the corner of my eye, saw the smile that brightened her face and guessed what was coming. And indeed I was right, as Mark announced that not only were he and Sara moving into the apartment upstairs the first of the year, they were engaged to be married.

"I couldn't wait until Christmas morning," he said.

"And I couldn't wait to say yes," Sara said, joining her new fiancé atop the bar. They hugged and kissed amidst a chorus of drunken cheers.

As the crowd quieted down and the two of them hopped off the bar, the crowd encircled the happy couple, Martha taking the lead. I took a step back, found Cynthia coming up to me. Said she was going to take Janey back to her place.

"Stay and enjoy yourself, Brian. Janey can stay with me and Brad tonight, and if she wants she can even invite Junior over. We've had a nice chat, the three of us. Bradley doesn't mind— when does he, the saint. It would be good for us to have a house with a couple of kids near Christmastime, you know? That will give you more time with your friends and your sister. Rebecca is quite a character, Bri, I can't believe you're related to her."

"I sometimes wish I weren't."

"I think she's been flirting with Chuck all night."

"Case in point."

"I think he's completely in the dark about who she is, too, isn't that a riot?"

We shared a hearty laugh over that. Imagine Chuck's expression when he found out the sexy lady in the slinky dress was related to the man he despised.

Before I could give my blessing to this sudden sleepover, I pulled Janey aside and asked her if she was okay with it.

"Yeah, don't worry, Brian, you have other people to take care of tonight."

Her words stung me deep inside, as though I had anyone more important to worry over or to take care of. She was my life and my world, and she was drifting away from me. With tomorrow being Christmas Eve, I felt uncontrollable fear grip my heart—the hoped-for joyous holiday I had dreamed of wasn't happening. Just the reverse, actually, and there seemed nothing I could do to stop it.

"Sure, have a good night. I'll see you tomorrow," I said, watching as Janey went out the door with Cynthia and Brad, Junior happily trailing behind them. Turned out they'd already checked with my sister. Rebecca hadn't had a problem with the arrangement, and I suspected she was gearing up for a night of partying. *Please don't hook up with Chuck Ackroyd,* that was all I hoped for. As for me, the party mood had seeped out of me. I tossed down my apron in frustration.

Mark had command of the bar, and Gerta offered to help him out. She had a lot of stamina tonight, and I was happy she had embraced the day with such gusto. A tribute to George for sure.

"Go ahead, Brian, you look exhausted," she urged me.

I left the tavern ten minutes later, Rebecca and John and Anna in tow, my past life like a sudden invasion inside Linden Corners. We did not go directly to the farmhouse. Instead I drove them out toward the highway, parking at the edge of the open field where we could see the giant windmill in the beams of our headlights. Even though the snow continued to fall and the air was cold, I asked them all to sit on the hood of their cars and "just wait." I went running across the field, quickly unlocked the front door of the windmill, and finally flicked on the light switch. I sent a silent apology to Annie, hoped she hadn't been too cold. Suddenly the world was lit with hundreds of bright white lights, and I dashed back to rejoin my friends and my sister, all of whom were awed by the magical sight before them. Tonight the sails spun, the falling snow like chilled fireflies dancing in the glow.

"This is my place, where I come to think. The windmill is where I can find Annie, and believe it or not, she helps me. In fact, it was Annie who dubbed this place atop my hood, as I gazed at the windmill, 'Brian's Bluff.' I feel the power of the sails. From here I think I can handle anything, that nothing in the world can stop me. I've never shared my bluff with anyone else, not even Janey. Just Annie, and now you, all of you who are so important to me."

"It's beautiful," Anna said, the others nodding in agreement.

"Not bad, Windmill Man," John said. He'd heard others call me that tonight.

"It's nice you've found where you belong, Brian," Rebecca said, a wistful, envious tone to her voice.

In the dark night, the light illuminating our faces, I fought back tears. But the quiver in my voice gave me away, and for a moment I felt the warm embrace of my friends, my family. But they weren't enough, not tonight. What I most wanted to hear was Janey's vibrant laughter, feel her joyous charm. I wanted Annie, too, to hear her voice, one that would help see me through the next days in my life. Neither seemed possible, and I just stared forward at the remarkable vision of the shining windmill, wishing I could change things. As I watched the windmill's giant sails turn and turn and turn in the night's breeze, I imagined the swirling wind catching my wish, and maybe, hopefully, granting it.

CHAPTER 25

The next day was Christmas Eve, and so my surprise overnight guests, John and Anna, Rebecca and Junior, departed around noon. All had their own plans and their own holidays to enjoy. In fact, they were all headed for New York, the new lovers expected at Anna's family's house for a traditional Italian feast, my sister and her son planning to celebrate the holiday by eating in nice restaurants and taking in a Broadway show. "We don't do traditional Christmases," Rebecca explained, standing before her sleek black BMW.

"Do you do this every year?" Janey asked.

"Since the divorce," Junior replied.

"Five years," Rebecca remarked.

"Then it is a tradition—yours," she instructed them. "That's what Brian taught me."

Well-spoken, I thought, proud of the way Janey and Junior had taken to each other. The two of them had returned to the farmhouse early this morning, joining us all for a big breakfast, and lots of whisperings about what gifts they hoped to get. Then they exchanged e-mail addresses so they could keep in touch. The advances of technology would not be denied in Linden Corners; the outside world could not be ignored. But both Rebecca and I were pleased that the two of them had gotten along so well. Maybe our distant family had taken a step forward, thanks to the power, the commonality of childhood.

I hugged Rebecca and reminded her about this solemn day for the Duncan family. My request was simple. "Remember Philip."

"That's why I came to Linden Corners, so we both could."

Thankfully she hadn't noticed the absence of my ornament on the tree.

Janey and I watched both cars pull out of the driveway. She waved one last time and then, when they were out of sight, staring up at me, she announced, "I like Junior, he's very nice when you get him to open up. His mother embarrasses him a lot. But I think he liked that we became such instant friends." Her eyes sparkled like diamonds. I bent down and embraced her.

"You did a very good thing, Janey—I'm proud of you. From all Rebecca has told me about Junior, he doesn't make friends too easily. So it must have been a nice surprise for him to have such an instant rapport with you. Though it hardly surprises me. Look at you and me, right? We clicked from the very moment we met."

"Junior just needed someone to pay attention to him, to listen to him. Conversation . . . communication, it's very important."

"Yes, it is," I agreed, trying to keep an edge from creeping into my voice.

A sudden cloud crossed her face, and gone was our happy moment. "I need to go back to Cynthia's now. She and I have some last-minute holiday details to take care of. Bye, Brian."

To hear Janey say good-bye to me cut deep. But I let her go without another word, mostly because I feared my voice might fail me. Janey's comment about needing attention and the importance of communication reawakened my paranoid feelings, not that they were sleeping too deep down inside me anyway. What I couldn't be certain of was whether the meaning behind her words was directed at me. Time and attention to Janey had never been a concern before, something that had never been questioned or been at issue. Given her mood shifts and the unspoken gulf that existed between us, though, given the fact that today was Christmas Eve and those hidden fears of her could have bubbled to the surface, anything was possible.

My impulse was to run after Janey and have that talk now, but in the end I left her alone. Instead, I went back inside and called Cynthia to explain that I was going to run a few errands. "No problem, Brian, Janey will be fine here."

As I headed out of town, a placard placed at the town's line reminded me about the children's pageant at St. Matthew's tonight. Their annual toy drive. So while I was out I picked up a last-minute gift to place under the tree at the church. All of my Corners friends were expected to attend the seven o'clock vigil mass, and for a moment I heard Father Burton's reminder rattle in my brain. It was a special celebration for the children of Linden Corners, one Janey had taken part in as long as she could recall. It was another long-standing village tradition, Gerta once informing me that "George and I took our four daughters every year while they were growing up. The mass is wonderfully inspiring. What good it does for our souls to offer comfort to those less fortunate." Gerta was planning to attend, as well, since she explained only one of her four daughters was coming home for Christmas, and in fact she said, "Viki and Dave and the kids will arrive late on Christmas Eve." As I ran my errands and fought against the crowds desperate for those ideal last-minute gifts, I found myself looking forward to the mass and being at Janey's side. I was gone nearly two hours, and then, thinking Cynthia had other things to do than taking care of Janey, I drove directly to her home. Brad answered the door.

"Hey, Bri, what's up?"

"Oh, I just came to pick up Janey."

"Really? She's not here."

There had been only one car in the driveway, so I assumed that Cynthia had taken Janey with her.

"Cyn did go out, but not with Janey. She wasn't even here when I got back from the office. Half day," Brad said, running a hand across his unshaven jaw. Guess he had that desired time off from the law firm now, he wasn't usually so casual. "That's real strange, Bri. We told Janey to call you, you know, make sure you were home. She told us you were."

Which meant wherever Janey had really gone off to, she was unsupervised and alone, and worse, she'd arranged it that way. A level of panic I'd never before felt surfaced in me, and I reacted with gut instinct. I raced back to my car, yelling out, "I'll call you when I find her," then peeled out of the driveway just as Cynthia was approaching it. From behind the wheel her eyes widened in surprise, but I kept driving, figuring Brad could explain what was happening. Time was precious to me, and I had to find Janey. Two long minutes passed before I was back at the farmhouse, running inside the house, calling out, "Janey, Janey, are you here?" But there came no reply other than the hollow echo of my own voice. Even though I knew the house was empty, I still did a thorough search from basement to attic and everywhere in between just to be certain. She was nowhere to be found. I stood in her room, feeling absolutely helpless. An idea hit me and I quickly dropped down and peeked my head under her bed. The cardboard box was gone. Just then the phone rang and I ran to my bedroom, grabbed it on the third ring.

"Janey?"

"I guess that means you didn't find her," I heard Cynthia say.

"No. Cyn, did anything happen while she was over at your house?"

"Nothing that I can think of. All we did was wrap some gifts. She seemed happy. You know, she seemed like herself."

Cynthia would know.

"Thanks," I said, hanging up without saying good-bye.

Redialing, I called the Baker home in the hopes that Ashley's mother answered. Instead, I heard Ashley herself on the other end, and when I told her who was calling I imagined that horrible little tongue of hers.

"Have you seen Janey?" I asked her.

"No, Brian, she's not here. She's mad at me anyway, so there."

And she hung up on me.

For a moment I wondered why Janey would be mad at her best friend. What was going on inside that little mind of hers? Could Ashley have been jealous of Janey's newfound friendship with Junior—they had spent most of the party talking, and maybe Ashley had gotten mad about that. It was the only rational explanation. Was their argument the reason behind Janey's disappearance? But the why could wait, the where was what took precedence.

Back down in the kitchen, I tried to think of where Janey might have gone off to—and on Christmas Eve of all days.

"Janey, where did you go?" I asked aloud.

Surrounded by constant reminders of Annie—her windmill knickknacks that ranged from salt and pepper shakers to coffee mugs and the clock upon the wall that ticked loudly—inspiration hit me. I ran from the house without my coat, noticing that the snow had begun to fall again, big wet flakes that clung to my sweater. I made my way down the hill to the windmill, hoping I had guessed right. We all have our special places where we can hide from the world. I had shown my friends Brian's Bluff. For Janey, the windmill was her happy place because it was where she felt the closest to Annie. Annie, too, had felt so safe from her troubles inside those wooden walls.

The front door to the windmill was locked, and I hadn't brought my keys. I remembered the spare key Annie had always kept tucked under the tower—for emergencies. I reached down and grabbed hold of the key, had the door unlocked in seconds. I flipped on the lights and looked around. Catching no sight of Janey, I called out her name anyway. Again, there came no reply, unless you counted a slight scuffling sound against the floor. Like shoes scraping against wood. Aha, she was upstairs in the studio. I took the steps two at a time, and when I reached the second level, Janey's shadow crept into my sight. She was pressed against the far wall, as though she was trying to escape from me. Her lips were quivering, and not from the cold.

"Hey," I said. "You okay?"

She didn't respond. Deciding not to approach her, I kept my distance by sitting down on the floor near the staircase. An offensive move, because there was no way she could get past me now in the unlikely event she tried to run. What-

ever had been eating away at her these past few
weeks, it was all going to come out now, that
much I was certain. Because it was almost
Christmas and because she was Janey and I was
Brian and together we were an unbeatable team.
This was supposed to be our first holiday together, a perfect holiday. Instead it continued
to spiral out of control.

"You want to tell me what's wrong?"

"Nothing. I'm just visiting Momma."

"Janey, you lied to Cynthia and Brad. You
told them that I was home, when you knew perfectly well that I wasn't. I told you to wait at their
house until I returned," I said, the fear in my voice
overpowering my firm tone. "Which meant you
were here all by yourself, and you know you're
still too young for that, sweetie."

"You can't tell me what to do—you're not my
father."

Ooh, I believed we had hit a nerve. This was
good, a verbal jab that hinted at progress.

"I know I'm not your father, Janey, never in a
million years would I think I was. But I am here
to look after you. I'm here because I want to
look after you."

"For now," she said.

"For now? What's that supposed to mean?
Where is it you think I'm going?"

"Home."

"I am home, Janey—the farmhouse is my
home. You are my home."

"For now," she repeated. "You know, until
you get tired of living here. And then you'll go

back to New York and be with your friends, because that's what you want. You just came to Linden Corners by accident."

"Accidentally, yes, but also on purpose," I said, hoping she would remember the strange juxtaposition of words from an earlier discussion. "And I love living here. The life I had in New York, sure, I had some fun times. But some of my memories, they weren't always good. Some days I woke up and had to wonder what I was working toward—sure, I had a good job and probably would have been very secure moneywise. But would I have been happy? I mean, truly happy and fulfilled? Not the way I am here, with you. Janey, your momma and I didn't ask to fall in love—in fact, we resisted it. Fate had another plan, and so she and I started to think about a future together."

"That's what you always do, Brian. Momma wasn't anyone special to you," she said.

I was taken aback, not only by the words but by the violent force she issued them with. As though Janey truly believed them. What could have given her such a ridiculous idea that Annie hadn't been important to me, that I hadn't loved her?

"You wanted to marry that Lucy girl, the one you loved from high school. That's what Rebecca said, and even your mom. And then John told me all about that woman Maddie. You were going to marry her, too, you even bought her a ring. And you never married either one of them, so why would you have married Momma? You could always find another woman to love and marry—because that's what everyone wants to do, get married. Look at Mark and Sara, maybe John and Anna—they'll probably get married. And so will you, and when you do you'll leave me."

"Oh my God, Janey," I said, my heart beating wildly. "Oh no, that's not true, not true at all." Tears had welled up in my eyes and I tried to wipe them away, to no effect, because more quickly showed up until it became a steady stream. Still, I couldn't wallow in my own tears. I needed to find a way to soothe Janey's wounded feelings, to ease her mind. Her lips were trembling and she further retreated into herself, arms encircled around her small body like a protective cocoon. Emotionally she had closed herself down. Somewhere out there, in my mind or in Annie's spirit or riding the current of the wind, existed wondrous words that would open her up again, return to me the infectiously happy Janey Sullivan I'd known. I hoped I could find them.

"Janey, it's true that I had hoped to marry Lucy—but I was very young then and so what did I really know about love? My life hadn't really taken shape. I needed to discover myself and my world, a life beyond Lucy. So with John's help I moved to New York and eventually I met Maddie. At that time in my life, Maddie and I wanted the same thing and we thought we could find it together. We had a plan. But as you get older, you realize what might have once been important no longer is. What matters most are the people in your life, not your achievements. When

I left New York, my life changed again, and I found myself looking for that something special; maybe that someone special. Maybe even beyond special—someone so great and so wonderful that I'm not even sure there's a word to describe them. With Annie—your momma—I thought I had found that person. But really, who I had found was you. Janey, that day at the windmill, I count it as one of the luckiest days of my life. It changed my life. You changed my life—for the better, and for always." I paused in an effort to collect my thoughts, wondering if this hidden insecurity of hers had led her to hide my ornament. Was it really that simple? "Janey, do you know why I took you to my parents' house for Thanksgiving? And why I took you to New York to see the tree?"

"Because you miss your home."

"Definitely not. No, sweetie, I took you there because I wanted to show you who I was before I came to live in Linden Corners," I said. "To share a part of my life with you. So you could know me better."

By this time my confession had her crying and the distance between us be damned, I went to her side and I held her and she held me, her sobs muffled because she was pressing so tight against me. I soothed her soul, I smoothed her hair, and I kissed the top of her head, and I assured her that everything was okay, rocking her, rocking her, never wanting to let her go. Still, I was searching inside me for one last piece of inspiration, solid proof that could finally settle Janey's tender fears. Surrounded by Annie's things, her paintings and her easel and her brushes, the very essence of her soul, I realized exactly what I needed to do.

As her tears subsided, I said to her, "Janey, do you remember your momma talking about a special place of hers?"

She nodded, sniffling at the same time. "Right here, Brian, the windmill."

"Well, yes, that's right, she always had the windmill. Except, I mean, the place she found before she became known as the woman who loved the windmill. Before she had even met your father."

Janey was thinking hard. Suddenly she got up from the floor and wandered over to Annie's drawer full of paintings. She started flipping through them one by one until she came to the particular one she was clearly looking for. Proudly she displayed a beautifully rendered painting of lush colors as vibrant as Janey's dancing eyes. It had been drawn from atop a hill, an illustration showing the mighty Hudson River and its environs, the lovely sky that hovered above it, the billowy green landscape that encased it.

"Momma liked the river, it's where she went to think."

"That's right. How would you like to go there now?"

"But Brian, I don't know where it is. Momma never took me. She told me once that she never took anyone there. Besides, only she could ever find it."

"That's where you're wrong, Janey, because she took me there once, and it was a very special moment for us," I said. "And today—Christmas

Eve—I'm going to take you. You can be even closer to your momma, how's that for a gift?"

Janey's sparkling eyes were alive with sudden wonder and delight, brighter now than any collection of lights could power, even those that cradled the windmill itself. And what were those eyes saying to me? That there were discoveries yet to be made, gifts still to come.

CHAPTER 26

Four o'clock in the afternoon on Christmas Eve, nightfall would soon settle over Linden Corners. Snow was continuing to float down from the sky in an endless flow of white confetti, and from what the weather reports indicated, it would most assuredly be a snowy white Christmas. In the past hour alone, while Janey and I had talked and talked inside the windmill, an inch of fresh powder had accumulated on the roads, making conditions less than ideal for driving. I had almost considered not going, but this was too important. If Annie had taught me anything, risk took second place to love. I'd assured Janey that she could visit Annie's Bluff—as I had dubbed it this past summer, the precursor to her naming my own Brian's Bluff—and nothing would stop me. Not rain nor sleet nor . . .

Janey and I had bundled up against the elements, and then hopped into the car. One last trip awaited us before the holiday could truly commence.

"Brian, are you sure you know how to get to Momma's special place?"

"Yes," I said, though in this wintery mix maybe I wasn't 100 percent positive. It had been a warm summer's day when Annie and I had gone there, a picnic in the trunk, romance on our minds. I would have to trust my instincts and listen to the wind.

Annie's Bluff was located atop a high hill that provided magnificent vistas of the Hudson River and the surrounding valley. For some people, this place was just one of many views of the river, offering up nothing particularly thrilling. There were many such views along the expansive waterway. For Annie, though, it had held such significance because it was where she had found direction in her own life, the place she'd come to for answers when things weren't going her way. And it was also a place she had shared with only one other person—me, done so at a time when neither of us knew what we would eventually mean to the other. Time had come to pass this secret on to the next generation.

So I parked the car at the base of the hill, just off the side of the road. Then, I took hold of Janey's mittened hand and helped guide her up a snow-covered path. At some places the drifts were nearly as tall as she, and I lifted her over them as though we were playing a game. I heard her familiar giggle and knew instantly this was the right thing to do. I had my Janey back.

We emerged from a thick cluster of trees into

a snowy clearing. Where once upon a time sunshine had dappled down on a pair of picnickers, today only the wind and snow welcomed this intrepid duo. But the wind powered the windmill and the great mill was our friend, and so there was nothing to fear from the whistling winds that, up on the hill, were strong enough to knock over a tiny girl. I held tight to her as she gazed out at the sight before her.

Below us wound the grand waters of the Hudson River, ice floes making their way down the river, crashing against its banks. A lone barge trudged through in the wintry storm, a light guiding its way along the dark waters. We waved to the passing boat, doubting we could be seen from this high above. But an echoing sound shook the sky as the captain sounded his horn—a lonely foghorn that rippled across the wind, calling to us Janey waved again as she went dashing along the bluff, dancing atop a large rock that sprouted up from the ground. I held her hand again, careful of the ice that coated the slippery stone.

"Oh, Brian, it's so pretty up here, I feel like I'm on top of the world. That's why Momma loved it so, isn't it?" Janey asked, her eyes on fire, marveling at the sight before her. "I bet on some nights you can see the moon, practically even touch it. That would be my wish. Because that's where Momma is, close to the moon and the heavens."

"That's a nice wish, Janey," I said. "Always remember to express your wishes because I know they can come true."

As she gazed down at me from her perch on

the rock, I expected to see a joyful child at my side. Instead I saw the worry return to her face, wrinkles crinkling her freckled nose.

"What's wrong, sweetie?"

"I'm sorry, Brian."

I lifted her off the rock, returning her to solid ground. I bent down and hugged her tight. "There's nothing to apologize for, Janey. But I do want you to remember that whenever anything is troubling you, you have to tell me. Never be afraid to tell me anything. I made a promise to your momma that I would always be there for you, and that's true every day, every minute. When you're happy and when you're sad, when you're sick or when you just want to sit quietly by yourself. All you have to do is tell me how you're feeling. Maybe what I need to do is make you that same promise. And there's no better place to make that promise than here upon Annie's Bluff, with a big open sky before us so your momma can look down and listen and see the magic that she created."

And, amidst the drifting snowflakes and cool night wind, that's exactly what I did. Warmth spread directly from her wide smile to my aching heart, winter and its chill having absolutely no effect on us.

"So," I said, "I think Christmas is coming. We have much to celebrate."

She paused. "Brian, can I tell you something?"

"Of course you can."

"Am I too young to babysit?"

My face must have showed my confusion. "Yes, I think so."

"Oh," she said, her face crumpling at the disappointment.

"You want to tell me whose baby you'll be sitting?"

"I can't, not yet."

"Why is that?"

She grinned and giggled like a girl who had unwrapped one of her Christmas gifts too early. "Because I'm not supposed to know."

CHAPTER 27

With the snow continuing to swirl and the wind picking up, the ride home turned treacherous, mostly because the plows hadn't come by and the roads were growing slick with ice. Maybe the snow was falling too fast for the plows to keep up, or maybe this was the way Christmas was supposed to look in Linden Corners. It was nearly six o'clock when we arrived at the farmhouse, just enough time to spare for us to grab a quick meal and get changed before attending the children's vigil mass at St. Matthew's. I sent Janey to put on her prettiest dress of crushed red velvet, while I went to put on a suit. After tying the tie, I knocked on her door and asked if she needed help.

"Maybe with the bow I want to wear in my hair," she said from behind the closed door. "I'll come down in a moment."

I checked my watch, saw that it was six twenty. "Let's go, let's go."

Back downstairs, I retrieved the gift I'd purchased for placement under the St. Matthew's Christmas tree and went outside to put it in the backseat of the car. Didn't want to forget that. When I got back inside the house, Janey was standing beside the tree, looking positively aglow in that velvety red dress. She shimmered against the burst of colorful lights. There was only one thing wrong with this picture, her quivering lips. Fear once again stabbed at my heart.

"Hey, what's wrong, sweetie?" I asked.

"I'm sorry, Brian," Janey said, practically crying now as she withdrew from behind her back the box that had once contained my family Christmas ornament. "I'm so, so sorry," she repeated and then she broke down into great heaving sobs that sent her little body shaking. My God, the fear she must have been holding inside her. Forgetting about the box, I took Janey into my arms and held her, comforted her and soothed her, wishing there were magical words that could wipe away the hurt that lay before us.

"It's okay, Janey, I'm not mad . . . I could never be mad at you," I said.

She was still sobbing, and I grabbed a tissue and wiped her eyes.

"Why, Janey, why did you hide it from me?"

She was still weeping but she was trying to talk, too. "I . . . I didn't, Brian, I didn't even know where it was . . . not until yesterday. Junior found the box under my bed when we were playing hide-and-seek in my room this morning. But the box was empty, Brian, I swear. The ornament was gone, but I never took it, honestly. I know it means so much to you, so I had to figure out what did happen to it. It couldn't have just disappeared on its own."

Her words struck deep at my heart, so much so I felt it bleed. All these weeks I'd been consumed with why Janey had taken it and why she wouldn't confess to hiding the ornament, and now I was faced with the undeniable truth: she wasn't responsible for its disappearance. She never even knew it was gone. My God, how could I have thought Janey would do such a thing? How easily I had assigned blame and then not done anything about it. Trust was a delicate bond, any wavering of it could bring disaster, suspicion . . . guilt ate at me. As I readied to listen to Janey's explanation, a sudden sadness gripped at me. She couldn't be so upset for having found just the empty box; she must have found the ornament as well. Which meant there was another problem—and I sensed that I wasn't going to like what it was. I opened the lid of the box. And that's when I saw the beautiful blue glass ball in pieces, shards as shiny as ever, like thousands of shattered stars fallen from the sky.

"Ashley took it, Brian. That first day I showed it to her, I told her I was jealous that you had such a pretty ornament and I didn't. When I told her everyone in your family had one, she said that just meant I wasn't part of your family.

So she took it—she said she was just trying to be my friend. When Junior found the box, I knew Ashley had to have it. And I also knew I had to get it back, so I went running off from Cynthia's and went to Ashley's house and took it back. That's why I was gone."

"So Ashley broke it?" I asked. No wonder that kid had been sticking her tongue out at me, she'd manipulated Janey into thinking she and I weren't family. Heck of a way to be a friend.

"No, Brian, it wasn't Ashley . . ."

"Then who?"

"Me. Oh, Brian, I broke your ornament. On the way home, Brian, oh, Brian, I dropped it."

She began to cry again. Quickly I set the box down and I took Janey into my arms once more, trying to assuage her fears and her guilt. How horrible she must have felt. "Oh, Janey, it's just a trinket, it's not important. It's just something to put on the tree, to see once a year. Just . . . just something from my past. You know you're who really matters, okay, sweetie? Sure, I'm upset that it's broken, but I don't blame you. How could I?"

"Brian, will you tell me about the ornament sometime? Junior told me a little about your brother, Philip, but I don't know what he has to do with your ornament. I want to know about your Christmases past, about your traditions. Will you tell me about Philip?"

I nodded, a wistful smile developing on my face as I wiped away my own tears. "Sure," I said. "When the time is right. But right now, we've got to get to church, okay? Father Burton will be very disappointed not to see you in the children's pageant."

A hint of color had returned to her cheek.

"Brian, are you mad at me?"

"No, Janey, I told you I could never be mad at you, and I mean that from the bottom of my heart," I said. We'd endured enough emotional strife for one day. "I'm sorry for all that's happened, Janey, between us. I guess the holidays can be pretty stressful, right?"

"I'm exhausted," she said, her body letting out a heavy sigh.

Her use of a big word actually had me laughing aloud. "So, what do you say, can we call it even, start fresh? We'll go to church, then we'll come home and begin our Christmas."

"So you're not going anywhere?"

"The only place I'm going is anyplace you're going," I said.

She scrunched her red nose at me. "Everyone calls you Brian Duncan Just Passing Through," she said.

"It's just a silly nickname," I said. "But how about we create a new one, huh? I'm Brian Duncan, Right Where I Belong."

"I like that one," she announced.

Okay, it was time to get ourselves to church before they started without us. She handed me the red bow and I affixed it to her hair and then pronounced her perfect. "Absolutely perfect." She giggled, and I finally felt like she was once again the Janey who had saved my life.

"Come on, then, we can't be late for Christmas, right?"

"Nope," she said.

As we headed back out into the snow and into the cold, starry night, I found myself smiling. Anticipation ran through me. For the first time in weeks, I was actually looking forward to our first celebration together. As the wind swept past us, I just knew there were still some surprises left in this holiday.

CHAPTER 28

According to the wooden sign posted at the village limits, the population of Linden Corners was 724 people, and give or take a couple dozen, it seemed as though everyone had turned out to celebrate Christmas with their families and with each other at St. Matthew's, a testament to the sense of community that I had felt from the very moment I stepped into its environs. Of course, folks from some of our neighboring towns came, as well, since the St. Matthew's Children's Christmas Pageant, I'd been told, was famous in these parts. St. Matthew's sanctuary was decorated with three trees that towered upward to the vaulted ceiling, all of them alight with sparkling white lights, their gleam caught in the flickering candles positioned atop the altar. A manger scene was set before the altar, the Baby Jesus not yet resting in his waiting cradle. And all around us, the smell of incense and the scent of pine re-

minded us all that Christmas was finally upon
us. Gerta sat at my side and Cynthia and Bradley
were in the row behind us and lots of other familiar faces filled the pews, parents who waited
with anticipation for the start of the mass, eager
to see their children process up the middle
aisle.

The adult choir began to sing "O Come All Ye
Faithful," the triumphant blast of an accompa-
nying trumpet raising the roof on our celebration. Then began the solemn procession with a
trio of altar boys, the lead carrying a large brass
cross, the other two with long, burning candles.
Behind them followed a cherubic young boy,
carrying in his hands the Baby Jesus, who would
be placed in the manger. Next came four adults
who would perform the readings and assist in
the Eucharist, and at last came the parade of
children, forty of them dressed brightly for the
holiday, the girls all dressed in red with crimson
bows in their hair and the boys with green ties
set against crisp white shirts and dark pants. Bringing up the end of the procession was Father Eldreth Burton, the kindly, wise pastor of our little
church. As the music swelled and the sound enveloped the church, the lead child placed the
Baby Jesus in the manger and the other children
placed their gifts beneath the trees until the
sanctuary was overfilled with an abundance of
giving.

For a moment I gazed up at the broken pane
of glass, recalling the shards of Mary and Jesus
hidden behind the boards. But today they were
dreamed into reality by our manger. Nothing

could keep them from our celebration. Turning back, I caught a glimpse of Janey near the end of the procession of children. With her color- fully wrapped present that she would place under the trees and her face lit with glee, she was a vi- sion among visions. I watched with unwavering pride, sharing in the joy of the other parents but envious of the larger bond they enjoyed, a blood connection. Still, Gerta squeezed my hand and remarked to me how wonderful Janey looked, "so healthy and filled with love. And we all know who to thank for that."

"All of us," I said quietly. "Annie included."

The children returned to their seats, and when Janey joined us I told her what a great job she had done. "So assured and professional," I said, "so grown-up." She kind of rolled her eyes at me, so I made a goofy grin.

"One of us has to be," she whispered to me.

That was my Janey.

The mass began, prayers were issued, read- ings read, songs filled the air, and Father Bur- ton delivered a short, powerful sermon about the real truth of Christmas and how the best gifts weren't to be found beneath any tree. I knew where mine was—the sweet little girl who sat between me and Gerta. A makeshift family, bonded by loss, forging ahead to the future.

As communion ended, Father Burton re- turned to his seat and like magic, the lights throughout the church were dimmed. Only the glow of candlelight flickered in the quiet of the church. The gentle sound of a piano could be heard, and moments later, the tender voice of a man's dulcet baritone. Not another sound could be heard throughout the church as the man sang a hymn called "Joseph's Song," a remarkable song whose lyrics spoke volumes to me, the words "Not of my flesh, but of my heart" seemingly directed right at me and Janey. The song came to an end, and the congregation sat in utter and absolute silence. All around us was embodied the power of Christmas, its message more clear to me on this occasion than any I could ever recall. Still, I thought of my family, of Kevin and Didi Duncan, and Rebecca and Junior, and then I added silent intention for Philip. The lights came back on as I wiped away my final tears of the night, and the mass concluded with a rousing "Joy to the World."

Afterward, I shook the singer's hand and thanked him profusely for his voice, his words, his lyrical song.

"I liked it, too," Janey said.

As the church emptied, I noticed Father Burton shaking hands with the departing parishioners. I told Gerta to hop into the line, taking Janey with her. I needed a moment, I told her. I went against the tide of the crowd, making my way forward to the sanctuary, kneeling before the manger. Glancing at the ceramic figurines of Mary and Joseph, at parents who had never asked to be but knew in their hearts that destiny had chosen them, I felt a sudden kinship with them. That's when I laid down one last gift, setting it inside the manger for safekeeping.

Janey and Gerta were waiting at the back of the church, Father Burton at their side.

"Beautiful service, Father," I said.

"Very glad to see you, Brian Duncan."

We shook hands and wished each other the merriest of Christmases. I nodded as we left, a lump in my throat.

"You okay, Brian?" Gerta asked.

"Yeah, I'm great."

"Don't say 'yeah,'" Janey instructed me, and even though the solemnity of the evening vigil still pervaded, I laughed aloud. My voice carried throughout the church and outside, where the wind billowed past and caught its sound.

We wished Gerta a wonderful Christmas with her daughter Viki and family, who were expected within the hour. Coming up behind were Cynthia and Brad, the two of them bundled tight against the enveloping cold. We all exchanged hugs, and I asked if we would see them later. I had invited them over for some holiday cheer.

"Actually, Brian, if it's okay, Cyn and I just want to spend a quiet Christmas, just the two of us," Brad said. He then gave his wife a look that could only be described as loving.

"Sorry to change the plans, Bri," Cynthia said, "but since this will be our last Christmas with just the two of us, we wanted to make it special."

"Sure," I said, but then realized I wasn't so sure. "Wait, what?"

Brad embraced his wife from behind, his hands resting on her belly.

"I just passed my first trimester," Cynthia said.

"Oh Lord, what a blessing," Gerta said, kissing Cynthia's cheek.

"Oh, Cynthia, Brad, I couldn't be more happy for you."

"We didn't want to say anything, until . . . well, until we were sure."

Cynthia, I knew, had suffered a couple of miscarriages early in her pregnancies. But now she assured us the doctor had said all was great. She was due in late May, she said, crouching down to look at Janey. "You may be a bit too young to babysit, but you'll be even more special for him or her. You'll be just like a big sister. What do you think of that, Janey?"

"I think I can teach your child a lot," Janey said. "After all, I've had such good practice with Brian."

Everyone laughed at my expense, and then we wished our holiday farewells to all. Brad led Cynthia down the snowy sidewalk and into their car, and they sped off in the darkness. A miracle had happened for them, and I felt pride fill my heart. We walked Gerta to her car, and soon she, too, was gone, leaving me and Janey in the parking lot, snow falling all around us.

"I told you," Janey said.

"Cynthia told you about the baby before tonight?" I asked.

"No, I just guessed."

"Come on, Know-it-all, let's get home and warm up."

Janey and I returned to our car and headed back to the farmhouse, the still-falling snow dancing in my headlights. Nearly a foot of snow had dropped already since this afternoon, and it showed no sign of stopping, not on this cold, blustery Christmas Eve night.

We listened to Christmas carols as we drank hot chocolate, and finally after she yawned, she remembered how "exhausted" she was. Good, Santa will be here soon, get to sleep, I said. First she had to place a few wrapped packages beneath the tree, telling me, "don't peek." Upstairs we went and she readied for bed. I considered reading to her *'Twas the Night Before Christmas,* "just like Momma used to do," but then decided upon another story. A new tradition, a new story.

"What's it about?" she inquired, cradling her purple frog.

"It's a story about the greatest gift of all," I said, settling onto her bed.

"Where's the book?"

"Oh, I don't need a book to remember how this one goes," I informed her, and then, at last, I began my tale. "Once upon a time, the most special person lived. His name was Philip and he decided one year that he wanted to give the best presents of anyone in his family, and so that's what he set out to do. He found these beautiful glass ornaments—red and blue, green and gold—and had one made for each person in his family. 'Put their names on it in glitter, I like that touch,' he told the glass blower, who had in his workshop silver glitter, the color of tinsel. Icicles," I added, which made Janey smile brightly. "And so that's what happened and Philip took them home. Then one Christmas morning the family awakened and under the tree were these pretty packages—just like the ones you placed downstairs—and the family opened them. There was a glistening red ball with the name *Kevin* on it, and a green one that read *Didi*, and then the gold one that spelled out *Rebecca* and the blue one that read *Brian*. They came with a note, each of them."

"What did the note say?"

"It said to remember him always—at each Christmas—and to always remember that Christmas means happiness and it brings families together. That's what he taught the family, Janey, and each year they remember his lesson when they place the beautiful ornaments on their tree. Ever since then, each of them has tried to live out his legacy—remembering that giving is greater than receiving."

"I like that story," Janey said. "Are you sad, Brian, not to have your Christmas ornament?"

I considered my answer before speaking. "What I've learned just today, Janey, is that I didn't need the ornament to remember Philip. I can honor him in another way, by passing along his story to those who will hear it. I call it 'The Greatest Gift.'"

Then I kissed her good night. She closed her eyes, and I watched as she drifted off to sleep.

Returning to the warmth of the living room, I sat in the recliner and stared at the glistening Christmas tree, knowing I still needed to brave the outdoors and retrieve all of Janey's presents from inside the windmill. I felt a yawn overcome me. I was exhausted from the activity of the past few days, the planning and execution of the tavern party and the emotional catharsis Janey and

I had gone through earlier today. I was spent and so I closed my eyes for the briefest of moments, thinking about the end of the story I hadn't told Janey, discovering my brother Philip asleep in his bed that Christmas morning. But he hadn't been sleeping; he would never again awaken. Philip Duncan had been twenty-three years old; I'd been eleven.

And beneath the tree, there had been no "Philip" ornament.

CHAPTER 29

"Brian, wake up! Santa didn't come, look, there's no presents!"

I jumped up from the recliner, surprised not only by Janey's voice but by what she was saying. Hadn't she just gone to sleep? I was just napping . . . right? Rubbing sleep from my eyes, it dawned on me that morning had indeed arrived. And not just any morning, but Christmas morning.

"Of course, he did, Janey, he must have . . ." When I looked down at the emptiness beneath the tree, my mouth closed. All that waited to be unwrapped beneath the tree were the gifts Janey had set out last night. Gifts she had wrapped for me. Words failed me as I realized I had failed Janey. For the past month my only concern had been giving Janey the most perfect Christmas ever, and here it had arrived and what had I done but fallen asleep before being able to set out her gifts. A boneheaded move on my part, for sure. Maybe Janey was right. Maybe she was the grown-up and I was the child. But, of course, there were gifts for her.

"They're in the windmill, all the gifts are there."

In her pajamas, her tiny self rolled her eyes as she placed hands on her hips. "That's where you're supposed to hide them, Brian—but on Christmas morning, they're supposed to be under the tree. That's Momma's tradition."

"Well, I guess we're going to have go get them," I said, a rare bit of inspiration on my part.

"Now, in the snow?"

"You want to wait until spring?"

"Not likely," she said.

Actually, Janey said she approved of my idea, it was the windmill after all, and so she went darting up the stairs and quickly dressed in her warmest clothes. I followed suit. As we stepped out onto the back porch, we saw that the snow had finally stopped sometime overnight and that glaring sunshine was brightening the white blanket of snow that covered the land.

"Wow, we got a ton of snow, Brian. How do we get to the windmill now? It's too deep for my little legs."

"An easy solution," I said, and went trudging through the deep drifts of snow, some as high as five feet because of the wind that had blown past the open field. I made my way to the barn and inside grabbed hold of the trusty red toboggan. I returned to the back porch, the sled trailing behind me, and asked Janey to hop aboard.

"Wait, not yet," she said.

Then she ran back inside the house, only to return with an armful of gifts.

"We can open them all in the windmill, Brian, that way Momma can see. She can have Christmas with us."

So maybe falling asleep last night had been the perfect thing, because what we ended up with was the ideal, small-town Christmas setting. Janey hopped aboard the toboggan, setting the gifts in front of her, and then I took hold of the rope and began making our way through the snow. Once we reached the hill, I sent Janey off, the sled racing downward with exponential speed, her gleeful laughter filling the air. I did my best to chase after her, but the drifts were too big and too difficult to maneuver through and more than once I fell forward. By the time we arrived at the windmill, I'd gone from Windmill Man to Snowman.

"You look like Frosty," Janey said.

"I feel frosty," I said, "and I think you need to, too." Then, with a devilish grin crossing my face, I pushed her backward into a large fluffy drift. A puff of white powder flew into the air as she hit the ground, downy flakes falling down on her face. "Now you're a Snow Girl."

Suddenly Janey began to move her arms and legs back and forth and in moments she had gone from a girl to an angel.

"No, Brian, I'm a snow angel."

"That you are," I said, and then I dropped down beside her.

"What are you doing?"

"Making a bigger angel." I began jerking back and forth, wondering what my friend John might think of me at this moment. He'd think the farm boy had finally cracked his eggs. Janey informed me that I was just making a mess and when I got up and looked at my handiwork, I had to admit she was right. Her angel looked perfect and graceful. Then there was mine, which looked an angel in the midst of a seizure. I suggested we open some gifts instead, only to find the entrance to the windmill was blocked by even more drifts. Not even the spare key would help us now, buried under all these feet of snow.

"This isn't the easiest Christmas I've ever had," Janey said.

"But it sure is fun, isn't it?"

I looked around at our surroundings, searching for a solution to our dilemma. Once last summer, in a moment of desperation I had reached the second level of the windmill by climbing its quiet sails, but today they were turning in the breeze, and even though their rotation was gentle I didn't want to risk injuring myself. So I returned to the barn, the snow continually dogging my progress and further delaying our morning celebration even more. But when I made my way back, I carried with me a ladder. I set it against the rear of the windmill, climbed to the catwalk with the gifts in my arms. Then Janey began her ascent and I grabbed hold of her gloved hands while she maneuvered under the low railing. We were something out of a children's picture book, a knight returning his princess to the tower after a grand adventure. From there I brushed some snow away from the outer door and soon we entered directly into Annie's studio.

I turned on a light, but we both left on our coats, since the cold had permeated through the wooden walls of the mill. There was no heat in this place. Remembering that I had stored a couple of blankets inside the mill, just as Annie had done, I retrieved one of them and set it on the floor. Janey sat down on the blanket and then I opened the closet and proceeded to place before her piles of gifts wrapped in shiny paper that showed reindeer and Santa and snowmen.

I sat beside her and watched as she began to unwrap each gift. Janey was a typical little girl in her likes, dolls with which you could play dress up, and so there was a new Barbie and several different designer outfits in which to dress her; there were some clothes, too, for Janey, and several stuffed animals, new friends for her favored purple frog. Finally there remained just two more gifts, and I presented the first one to her with excitement.

"This is from your past," I said.

"What is it?" she asked.

"Unwrap it and find out."

She began to tear at the paper. Underneath she revealed one of Annie's paintings, newly framed and protected by a glass covering. I had gone back and forth on which painting would be perfect, thinking maybe the one of Annie's

Bluff, thinking maybe one of the windmill. In the end, I settled upon the painting of a very young Janey cradled in the arms of Dan and Annie Sullivan, the two of them proud new parents.

"Thanks, Brian, I love this gift so much. It helps me remember, especially my father."

"We'll hang it in your room, okay?"

"That's the perfect place," she said, hugging me so tight I thought I might explode with emotion.

"There's one more gift, Janey."

"But you've already given me too much," she said.

Seeing her surrounded by the numerous gifts, perhaps she was right. I had spoiled her, but if ever a little girl deserved to be spoiled, well, here she was. So that's when I handed her the last gift. "This gift is from your future."

"Momma just used to say they were all from Santa Claus."

"I like to do things differently," I said.

"Tell me about it."

Still, she gazed up at me with wide, curious eyes, then returned them to the small, square box I'd placed in her hands. Gently she unwrapped the present, opening up the lid on the square box. As she discovered what lay inside that box, her mouth dropped with wonder and surprise.

"Oh, Brian . . ."

"Go ahead, take it out of the box."

And she did, and what she saw was her very own Christmas ornament, a shiny red glass ball, the name "Janey" lettered in silver glitter.

"Consider that one a gift from Uncle Philip," I said. "Just as I'm part of your family, you are now part of mine. And nothing can ever change that, not anymore."

Janey had no words to offer up, perhaps a first. I had to settle for a hug, one that lingered for minutes, and that was just fine with me. I could feel her sweet tears seeping through my shirt.

"You're welcome," was all I said.

Finally, with obvious care, she returned the ornament to the box. Then she informed me that it was my turn to open up my gifts. There were two boxes, the first of which contained a 3-D jigsaw puzzle called "The Spectacular Spinning Dutch Windmill," which Janey informed me "really spins" once you put it together. I told her what a special gift it was and how I looked forward to the two of us building the windmill, "Something we seem to be very good at." The second gift was a box of staples—"you know, for the staple gun. You used up an awful lot when you decorated the windmill with all those lights." I laughed at this second gift, treasuring the sentiment behind it.

"But those are just fun gifts, Brian. I wanted to get you something really special, and I asked Gerta and Cynthia and even John, when he showed up for the party. They all kept telling me you already had the gift you wanted."

"You," I said.

"Hey, that's what they said. But Brian, that wasn't enough, not for me. So the decision was all mine—to find the best gift in the whole wide world. So I got you something I think we'll both like." From the inside of her jacket she pulled out an envelope and handed it to me. "It's the other reason I disappeared yesterday from Cynthia's. I went to town all by myself—I know I'm not supposed to, but I just had to, Brian, I had to get this card from Marla's store. I knew she carried lots of cards. It was on my way home from Ashley's that I stopped there." She paused, momentarily looking away from me. When she returned, her eyes locked directly on mine. "That's when I dropped the ornament, Brian, when I was buying the card."

I looked at Janey with surprise at her ingenuity and at her boldness, her impulsiveness and at the tragic irony, too, of her tale. She must have been very determined to get me this particular card to have risked so much. So without further ado I opened the back flap of the envelope and withdrew the card. As soon as I saw the writing on the front, my lips quivered and a wave of emotion rippled up and down my spine. My eyes blurred with tears and I almost couldn't make out the words. But I could never forget them, though, because what it said was, "For My Dad, At Christmas." On the inside of the card she had written, "To my new Dad, Merry Christmas, Love, Janey." I was left without a single word on my tongue.

"I'm only eight and I have lots of growing up to do and I'm going to need help," she explained. "After I bought the card I came immediately to the windmill because I needed to ask Momma if it was all right that I have a new dad.

She's my momma and she always will be, and my father will always be my father. But you can have a dad, too, that's what I learned—Junior taught me that."

"Janey, you bought this card yesterday? Before we talked? But . . . you were so worried that I might want to return to my old life and get married. You thought . . ."

"Yes, Brian, that's what I thought. I'm a little girl, I'm going to think weird things sometimes. Besides, that's only what my head was telling me. My heart, though, it knew what to feel. I knew you were here to stay. So, will you, Brian, will you be my new dad?"

"I think I already am," I said.

With a squeal that echoed far and wide, Janey jumped into my arms and I didn't let her go, not for the longest time, relishing this moment with the little girl who on this most giving of holidays had given the best gift of all, her unconditional love and her great big heart. I couldn't believe this incredible gesture, this most wondrous and unimaginable sacrifice.

"Come on," I finally said. "Let's go hang your new Christmas ornament on the tree."

And when we did, Janey and I held it together and found just the perfect branch for it.

"Thanks, Dad," she said.

This time words failed me.

CHAPTER 30

The phone rang around noon. Janey was playing with her new toys, and I was still marveling over the card she had given me. I would treasure it forever, just as I would Janey herself. When I picked up the receiver, I heard Gerta say, "Merry Christmas, Brian." I returned the greeting and asked how her holiday morning had gone.

"Fine, just fine," she said, though her voice lacked conviction.

"Gerta, who's there with you?"

"Oh, I'm fine, Brian, just fine."

"Gerta?"

That was the second time she'd said those words, and they sounded rehearsed and hollow. As I recalled the constant snowfall of the night before, a sneaking suspicion crept upon me.

"Gerta, your daughter and her family couldn't

make it, could they? The snow stranded her at her home, didn't it?"

"I told her not to attempt it, the roads were horrendous. They still are."

"So you're alone?"

"I'm fine, Brian . . ."

"Yeah, I didn't believe you the first time you said it. Hang on, Gerta, it's Janey and Brian to the rescue."

"No . . . Brian, really the roads are too impass-able—don't chance it."

"I won't," I said.

"What are you plotting, Brian Duncan?"

"Oh, nothing much, but I might be just pass-ing through," I said, smiling as I replaced the re-ceiver. I called out to Janey that we had a special errand to run, she'd better get ready. Once again we bundled ourselves against the winter cold, once again we loaded a few presents onto the sled and Janey took up her position at the back of the red toboggan. I took hold of the rope in a repeat performance from this morn-ing, and then we were off.

The back roads hadn't been plowed; it seemed everyone was taking a holiday today. But that meant there were no cars to fuss with on the road, giving me and Janey and the red sled free rein during our travels. It was a two-mile trek to the Connors' home on the other side of Linden Corners, and we spent the time it took to get us there by singing Christmas carols, ending with "Frosty the Snowman" because that's how we felt and looked. We headed up

Gerta's driveway, glad to have finally made it. As we reached her porch, she emerged from the inside, a worried smile on her face.

"Oh, the two of you, get inside right now, it's freezing out there," she said, obviously delighted to see us. "Goodness, what am I going to do with you? I've been pacing my house for the last hour wondering what you were up to. You came all this way on the sled?"

"Yup, it was fun," Janey said.

"Completely worth it," I added.

"I think I better get that cocoa made," Gerta said, hustling us before a blazing fire in her living room. Her tree lights were on, and in the background I heard the faint sound of Christmas music. Hanging on the mantel were two stockings, one with her name, the other George. I felt a lump in my throat as I thought of Gerta awakening this morning, her first Christmas without George. But from what I could see, her spirits weren't dampened. Gerta and Janey were not uncommon when it came to rallying themselves; their enthusiasm for life far outshined their troubles. Or maybe it was their way to honor those they had lost.

"Hot chocolate sounds like a good idea," I said.

"With tiny marshmallows," Janey added.

"Absolutely, with tiny marshmallows," Gerta said with a great smile. "While I take care of that, Janey, there's a gift with your name on it waiting under the tree."

"Wow, more Christmas presents," Janey said, running to see what Gerta had gotten her. As it turned out, more Barbie accoutrements. Gerta and I had actually coordinated this.

We settled into the living room with our cocoa, and I lit some logs in the fireplace, where before long a refreshed fire crackled and a sweet warmth began to envelop the room. I passed Gerta her gifts, the first one more or less something to make her smile.

"New pie plates, why, Brian Duncan, whatever does this mean?" she asked, laughter in her voice.

"It means he likes your pies, Gerta," Jancy said.

"I bet you do, too," she said.

Janey giggled.

The second gift was another of Annie's lovely paintings, this one a scene of the village of Linden Corners in winter, the sign CONNORS' CORNERS evident in the background. Like Janey's gift, I had this one framed, as well.

"Oh, Brian, what a remarkable idea."

"It's from Janey, too, she's the one who suggested it."

"Momma liked to paint," she explained.

"It's just beautiful," she said. "I can almost picture George inside this world, happily toiling behind his bar."

Gerta then informed me it was my turn to open my gift. It looked like a shirt box but judging from Gerta's expression I believed she was trying to fake me out. Indeed, that proved to be the truth. There was no shirt inside the cardboard, just a folded piece of paper. I unfolded it and began to read. My eyes widened with genuine surprise. I gazed at Gerta and said, "Oh no, I couldn't possibly accept . . ."

"You will accept it, Brian, there's no debate."

What I held in my hands was a piece of the past. It was the property deed for the tavern—for the entire building, actually. I wasn't just a bartender; I was the owner of the bar and Mark Ravens's new landlord.

"Gerta, thank you—I don't know what to say. Your generosity . . ."

"Is unmatched by yours, Brian," she said, laughing. "My goodness, who else would pull a sled for two miles through five feet of snow just to make sure some old lady had company for Christmas? You did that without thinking, and that, Brian, is what makes you so special. Janey knows it, and so do I."

"This Christmas, it's been such a rewarding day already," I said. "I feel so rich."

"So does St. Matthew's Church," Gerta said.

"What do you mean?" I asked, surprised at the turn in the conversation.

"Oh, I think you know exactly what I mean, Brian Duncan Just Passing Through," Gerta said.

"Oh, we don't call him that anymore," Janey announced. "He's Brian Duncan Right Where He Belongs."

"Yes, indeed," Gerta said. "Seems St. Matthew's received the most extraordinary Christmas gift last evening—left there sometime after the vigil mass. Father Burton was retrieving the Baby Jesus figurine for the midnight mass when he discovered an envelope had been placed in the manger. An anonymous person had left a cashier's check for twelve thousand, five hundred dollars. A note was attached, asking that the money be used to help restore the stained-glass window that was damaged in last summer's storm."

"Huh," I said.

"More like wow," Janey said. "That's a lot of money."

"Yes, it is," Gerta agreed.

That's when I showed Gerta my Christmas present from Janey, the beautiful card. "Some of us received gifts that are priceless. Right, Janey?"

"Right, Dad."

A few minutes later, Janey went to set the table for our Christmas meal, and Gerta came and sat beside me, her voice soft.

"Your father gave you a check for twenty-five thousand, Brian. Can I assume you kept the other half?"

I shook my head. "I just couldn't," I said. "I donated it to something my parents will hardly object to, though. I sent the other check to the Philip Duncan Cancer Fund."

The snow returned that afternoon, and Janey and I remained at Gerta's, where she cooked the most delicious glazed ham dinner, and for dessert, rather than strawberry, she went with a peach pie, Annie's specialty. Surrounded by the two women who had most changed my life, the ever-sweet Gerta Connors and the irrepressible Janey Sullivan, my first Linden Corners Christmas came to a rapid close. For weeks I had struggled in my search for guidance, from the windmill and from Annie and from Father Burton and from all the people who made up this town called Linden Corners. I guess that wish upon the wind I made had been heard after all, because from tragedy had come such goodness, from the people who made my life so full and so rich, so complete.

Two families had shared their Christmas traditions, and in doing so had made new ones. But it had gone beyond new traditions, and instead what was formed was a new family, one that went beyond blood, one that was sealed with a powerful thing called love. Next year we would welcome life into our family, Cynthia and Brad's bundle of joy. We needed that, all of us. It was a gift from above, from the people whom we had loved and lost.

I had to wonder if somewhere among the stars Annie had maybe met my brother, Philip.

EPILOGUE

Theirs was a seemingly unbreakable bond, one that had been built by the power of the wind and by the presence of the mighty windmill. Today the windmill spun its special brand of magic, even as the uncertainty of a new year presented itself. On this night in December, the last one of the year, he found himself walking through the deep drifts of snow, venturing to the base of the windmill. It was here, on this eve of resolutions, he sought inspiration and knowledge and strength, all of which he would need to negotiate his way through the memories of a past that threatened to undo their fragile happiness. Because as wonderful as they were together, life hadn't always been easy, it came with daily challenges. But the coming year would prove that the two of them could get through anything.

"Annie, can you hear me?" he asked aloud, hoping the wind would carry his words forward, upward. This time he knew they would. *"I wanted to thank you, Annie. Christmas has come and gone. We missed*

you—Janey did with all her heart, I know that, because with everything we planned and everything that we did, always Janey would mention you and tell me about your traditions. I missed you, too, so much. You changed my life, first by entering it and second when you left it, but in the process you gave me the most wonderful gift ever, the gift of the future. Tomorrow a new year begins—we'll never forget the past and never forget you. The painting of you and Dan and Janey when she was a child, it hangs in her room and will forever and always. I think now we'll be able to move forward. We're still getting to know each other, and this past month we suffered our greatest challenge. When I last spoke to you, I wondered if I was enough for Janey. I think you answered that pretty well for me, and for her. What do you think?"

There was no immediate answer, not today. Snowflakes fell lightly, the wind was gentle and the sails spun slowly, as though the windmill itself could anticipate the quiet soon to descend on the tiny village of Linden Corners, on its residents and on its way of life. For Brian Duncan, this new year would be one of wonder, of new experiences. But that's what this past year had been about, and look how he had grown from all he'd gone through. He had little doubt the growing would continue, Janey would continue to teach him. So January was around the corner, the turning of the calendar page and the start of new chances.

"Annie, I took Janey to meet my parents. She met my sister and my nephew and she even met John, whom you never met and I always wished you had. He's a good guy, even if he still thinks I've become a farmer. Communication was never a strong point with my family, but Janey has opened up new possibilities *for me, for them. Just yesterday my parents called and said they would like to visit, perhaps this spring when the snow clears. Another new awakening for us all, thanks to Janey and her infectious charm. I'll show them the windmill and hopefully they'll begin to understand the choices I've made."*

There was another snowstorm headed for Linden Corners, for the entire Hudson River Valley region actually, and for a moment he imagined Annie's Bluff covered by snow, hidden from the world, to be discovered only by himself and Janey, and always together. Just then the wind picked up and the sails began to turn faster.

"You know, Annie, sometimes you're very quiet. Like the woman I met this summer. And sometimes—now—you make yourself known. Is there something on your mind?"

From the corner of his eye he saw Janey emerge over the hill. With her boots on, she made slow progress on her way through the drifts.

"Oh, I see, you're saying hello. Come to wish your daughter a happy New Year? That's what we all wish for, Annie, the happiest of them. I think Janey and I are on the road to having one, but know this, we're never far away. Call to us anytime. Oh, and if you meet a guy named Philip on your travels, tell him 'The Greatest Gift' lives on, that he lives on."

And the wind whipped past him again, the sails spinning faster for a moment. Soon, though, they quieted down, silenced once again.

"Come on, Brian," Janey said, "it's almost midnight."

So it was. He had lost track of time. Back at the farmhouse, his guests waited for him. He'd made the *decision to close the tavern tonight, he thought people should be with family, not alone at a bar, watching time slip aimlessly away. At the farmhouse were Cynthia and Brad, the two of them sharing their impending parenthood with them; Mark and Sara were there, too, the ring on her finger no better symbol of tomorrow. And Gerta, too, serving pie as always. They were all gathered in anticipation of the arrival of a new year.*

"Let's not go back, not yet," he said, the windmill still bright with illumination.

"Just us," she said.

"Just us," he said.

Janey stayed at his side, right where she belonged. Minutes later, the clock ticked past midnight and the year of the windmill ended. A new year had begun, its story not yet written, its fate yet to be discovered. There were always new stories to tell and new discoveries to be made in this happy village known as Linden Corners.

If you enjoyed A CHRISTMAS WISH,
you won't want to miss

A CHRISTMAS HOPE

By Joseph Pittman

Turn the page for a special excerpt.

A Kensington Trade Paperback On Sale Now

CHAPTER 1

NORA

"How come it's snowing . . . it's only October."

"Because, honey, we're in the thick of Upstate New York and in this neck of the woods they only have two seasons, winter and August."

"That makes no sense, one's a month and the other is a season."

No argument there. She nodded agreeably. "Welcome to Linden Corners."

The boy looked dubiously at his mother. "Am I going to like living here?"

Good question, she thought. Was she? Did she ever like it?

The drifting snowflakes falling all around the fire-red Mustang were only the first hint that she was nearing the tiny village of Linden Corners, but it wasn't until she crested over the rise in the highway and came upon the spinning sails of the old windmill that she knew she was truly home. Home, she thought, afraid to taste the flavor of the word on her bitter tongue. What other notion instilled such a juxtaposed sense of both comfort and failure? Being back here was reason enough to sigh, and not in a relaxed way. Her name was Nora Connors Rainer, and she wasn't pleased by any of this, not the snow and not the sight of that windmill, not to mention the idea of Linden Corners itself. Returning to the place of her childhood meant only one thing: Her adult life was an utter disaster, and given the fact that her car was overstuffed with her belongings—what some might call "baggage"—a jury would render a verdict within minutes of deliberating. Guilty, Your Honor, of grossly mismanaging her life, as well as that of her twelve-year-old son. She was a lawyer by trade, unable to even win her own case. How she wished she could just continue driving through the village, it was small enough it would only take a minute or so. A one-blink-and-you-miss-it kind of town.

There was also a sense of claustrophobia about the town, too, or so thought the worldly Nora, who had traveled the globe and seen many beautiful sights, now seeing the world spit her out from whence she originated. Just when she needed her street smarts the most, home was calling, the comfort and security and understanding that you could only find inside the walls of your parents' house, now just a mile away and creeping ever closer. No doubt a couple pieces of

her mother's famed strawberry pie awaited
them both. With the windmill now fading to
small in her rearview mirror, Nora felt her heart
beating with nervous anticipation. Home meant
many things to many people, but at this moment Nora needed its sense of reassurance.
Knowing those old walls came complete with a
supportive mother to hold you tight and tell you
everything was going to be just fine, her mind
told her maybe all would be okay.

But then she knew it wouldn't be, not ini-
tially.

Her homecoming would no doubt be seen as
an occasion for her mother. So she had to assume the house would not be empty, since the
sweet-natured Gerta Connors enjoyed having
company. And said company would ask questions, and said company would expect answers.
Suddenly Nora saw a houseful of guests, all of
them stuffing their faces with pie, their smiles
sweeter than sugar, but digesting gossip at her
expense.

"Please, do me this one favor and don't let
her have anyone over, I can't deal with . . . this,
not now," Nora said aloud. "Don't let her think
my homecoming is a celebration."

"Uh, Mom, are you talking to me?"

"Sorry, honey, Mom's weirding out."

"No kidding."

Her son's sarcasm, which had been coming
on strong in the past six months, actually produced a rare smile on her tight face. Normally
she'd reprimand him for his tone, but not
today. He'd earned the right to vent as much as

she deserved its wrath, she'd turned his life upside down. Still, Nora knew her mother, just as much as she recognized the friendly confines of Linden Corners, both the good and the bad. Having grown up here, she was well acquainted with the village's quirky tendency toward parties and parades, the happiest of holidays and heartspun happenings, her mother, Gerta, oftentimes at the center of planning the numerous, joyous celebrations. Heck, it was only the end of October and the fallen snow already had a layer of ice beneath this fresh coating of snow, no doubt the residents had a name for such an occasion. "Second Snowfall" or something cheekily homespun like that. Winter in this region came early, stayed often, and you needed the patience of a saint and good driving skills to navigate its literal slippery slope. This year, Nora herself would be like the ever-present season, setting up roost for some time to come, even she didn't know. She could one day decide to leave, then a storm inside her could erupt and she'd be trapped. Again. Nestled in the lush Hudson River Valley, cocooned from the outside world, she could easily lose herself.

That part she liked.

Of course cocooned was just a nice word for hiding.

Nora Connors Rainer and her one son, Travis, had left the flatlands of Nebraska five days ago, enjoying the long drive and each other's company, if not necessarily looking forward to their final destination. They could have easily flown to Albany, had the car shipped or just sold it and bought a new one when they arrived, but Nora wasn't ready to sell off everything from her past life. Call her shallow, but she'd worked too hard to buy her sporty red Mustang. Too bad she hadn't worked as hard at her marriage. But hey, a car allows you to just turn on the engine and steer it to where you wanted to go. A husband tended to have his own ignition, liked to drive by himself, go off on his own, embracing the unexpected surprises around winding curves. So then why was she the one on the open road, heading into the tiny downtown of a village whose future best existed in a rearview mirror?

Not that the village was all that empty at four o'clock in the afternoon. She recognized several stores like Marla and Darla's Trading Post—twins she'd gone to school with, inseparable then, business partners now, sisters forever and guarding the storefront, under the porch and seemingly oblivious to the snow, were two golden retrievers who lay quietly, sleeping the afternoon away in that lazy, entwined way shared only by our canine friends. Of course, too, there was the Five O'Clock Diner, run by the sharp-tongued, quick-witted Martha Martinson, plus the reliable Ackroyd's Hardware Emporium and George's Tavern, which she had known her entire life as Connors' Corners. It was where her father had happily toiled for much of his adult life. She'd heard about the renaming in e-mails and phone calls and how that wonderful Brian Duncan continued to honor George Connors's traditions and she'd seen pictures of the new sign, but the sight of it now made her heart ache for the loss of her father, for her still-living mother who had to live with the daily memories of her late husband.

But the store that most caught Nora's attention was darkened, a CLOSED sign posted on the locked front door. The building was in need of a paint job, flakes peeling off its sides. Elsie's Antiques it was called and had been for the better part of her life. But that was about to change.

Even in Linden Corners, change occasionally happened.

"Hey, Mom?"

"Yeah, baby?" Nora said, her eyes drifting away from Elsie's shop with reluctance.

"You know what today is?"

"It's Thursday, I think. Wait, what day did we leave . . . ?"

"No, not day. Today. It's Halloween."

Nora looked out her driver's side window and wondered how she had missed them. Too focused on seeing the village her way, she failed to notice how her son's eyes would view it. Seemed the sidewalks of the village were currently peopled with tiny ghosts and goblins, witches with straw brooms, vampires with fangs and tight abs, bums (though, truth be known, that last one might have not been a disguise), all of them carrying orange plastic pumpkins, winter coats unfortunately partly covering their clever costumes. Adults accompanied them to ensure nothing untoward happened to their ghoulish charges, or that they got too cold while out trick-or-treating. The allure of Halloween had lost its appeal years ago, just another foolish pseudo-holiday. She remembered dressing up as a ballerina when she was a kid; but heck, it's not like she played the part of a ballerina. People today, they tended to embody their costume rather than just simply wear it. As though everyone was starring in their own movie, stopping at makeup before stepping before the camera. While Nora may not like it, Travis always enjoyed planning his costume.

"Sorry. You were gonna be Batman this year, right?"

"Nah. Robin."

"How can you have Robin without Batman?"

"Dad was going to play Batman."

Well, that comment shut her up but good. And she felt worse than before, a sharp pain stabbing at her empty gut. Not only was Travis missing out on one of his favorite holidays, but he was missing it along with his father. She hated disappointing her only child—taking him from his home and school and friends, all he'd ever known, to return to . . . here. She looked again at the kids dressed in costume, one in particular covered in a white sheet with two eyelets. Ghosts indeed, they were all around, and not just on the sidewalks, but in the trunk of her car and inside her mind. Oh yes, those phantoms never left, did they? They never needed the arrival of a single day of celebration to come out and haunt.

"I'll make it up to you," she said.

"What, you'll be Batgirl?"

She smiled over at him, relieved to see he still had a streak of sweetness underneath all that almost-teenage sarcasm. "I promise to make the next holiday real special, okay, sweetie? I know how much you like Christmas, too."

"Uh, Mom?"

"Yeah, honey."

"The next holiday is Thanksgiving."

She actually laughed, loud enough to rattle the windows inside the car. The sudden release felt good, and at last she allowed her shoulders to drop. For Nora Connors Rainer, this new life they were starting here in Linden Corners, it was going to be harder than she envisioned. Good thing her mother was there to help, and not just with Travis's expected adjustment. Nora knew she needed all the help she could get.

"Oh, and one other thing?" Travis asked.

She was concentrating on the snowy roads ahead, yet she managed to sneak a quick look at her young son. She felt an overwhelming sense of love, knowing she would do anything to ensure a happy childhood for him. She knew how lucky she was to have him at her side. It might have been different.

"Sure, love, what's that?"

"Can you just call me Travis from now on? All that baby, honey, sweetie stuff," he said, "it doesn't suit the man of the house."

Nora's easy laughter from moments ago dissipated, like she'd opened the window and let her joy take to the cold air. Now she just wanted to cry.

How was it that her son was growing up when she wasn't?

* * *

She turned off Route 20, which served as the village's main artery, and wound her way up Green Pine Lane, remembering each curve of the road as well as she knew herself. When she caught sight of the old house, Nora felt herself retreat back to Travis's age, a helpless twelve-year-old girl with brown pigtails and hand-me-down clothes from her three older sisters and a sour, uncertain expression on her face. Only the hairstyle and clothes had changed. Oh, and her age.

Forty and moving back in with Mom.

Good job, Nora, she thought.

"Mom, I know you're still talking to yourself . . . even if I can't hear it."

"This is hard, Travis. Just give me a moment."

She pulled to the side of the road, tires crunching in the fresh snow. The house looked small, even though it had three floors, four bedrooms, and lots of space in the basement and attic. After all, her parents had raised four girls there—she the youngest, along with older sisters Victoria, Melanie, and Lindsay, so clearly the house had been big enough to accommodate them, big enough that if you wanted to hide you could. And Nora was a hider, even back then. Down in the basement or cuddled up on the old sofa, she could easily get lost in the fantastical world of whatever book she was reading, or the drama found in the pretend lives of her dolls. She wondered if her mother would insist that she take back her old room. Nora wasn't sure she could handle that, but also questioned where else she would hide. This was the first time she'd been back to the house since her father, George, had died, almost a year and a half ago. She took a deep breath. Yup, this was hard, harder than she'd anticipated.

"Okay, kiddo, you ready?"

"That's a new one."

"What is?"

"Uh, hello, kiddo?"

"Sorry, mother's instinct," she said. "Ready, Mr. Rainer?"

Travis just rolled his eyes.

"Got it, sorry, let's go," she said with another laugh; her emotions were a jumbled mess, there was no telling how fast her mood could turn. She guided them back onto the slick, snow-covered road, steeling herself for the final steps. It was just another three hundred feet before she would turn into the short driveway, their journey complete yet somehow also just beginning.

A blaring horn from behind caused her to slam on the brakes and that's when a loud smack jolted them forward.

"Shit," Nora called out, tossing the car into PARK.

They had been rear-ended.

"Mom!"

"Sorry, honey. Are you okay?"

"Yeah. Just surprised me is all."

"Okay, wait here, let me see what happened."

Nora unclenched her seat belt, not her teeth, as she made her way out of her prized car to assess the damage and to confront the dumb idiot who had crashed into her. What she saw was a battered old farm truck, two people up inside the high cabin. As she made her way toward the driver's side door, she stole a look at the back of her prized Mustang. The fool had taken out a brake light, left a small gash on the side bumper. She could see the bright red paint on the grille of the truck.

"Hey, look what you did," she said, pointing to the damage.

The man behind the wheel stepped out, closing the door behind him.

"What I did? You just pulled out, didn't even look to see if there was traffic."

"Traffic? In Linden Corners? Not exactly two concepts that go together."

"Nora?"

"Excuse me?"

"You're Nora, aren't you? Gerta's daughter."

Nora blinked away the snow that was falling in her face, clearing her eyes. Who was this farmer and why did he know who she was? She looked over at the other passenger in the truck, saw a young girl with a scrunched-up nose peering over the high dashboard, and that's when she knew who he was, knew who the girl was, and what they were doing here just a short distance from Gerta Connors's house.

"Brian Duncan," she said, placing her hands on her hips for effect.

"You recognize me?"

"No. But one and one in this case still equals four. I'm guessing that's Janey Sullivan in the truck. My mom talks about the two of you all the time."

"Small world, huh? She talks of you often, too, especially lately," he said. "We were just heading to your mother's house to pick her up to take her to the annual village Halloween party over at the community center. We call it the Spooktacular."

Nora allowed a knowing smile to cross her lips despite herself; she'd guessed it right. Linden Corners would never let a holiday pass by without some kind of celebration; like its middle name was "annual." "How nice. But I don't get your costume," she said, assessing his faded jeans, scuffed boots, and red flannel shirt. "You some kind of farmer?"

"Ha ha, no, I haven't changed yet. Janey in there, she's a windmill."

Of course she was, Nora thought.

"I'm sorry about your car," Brian said, "but you did just pull out without warning. I tried to warn you, but . . . you know, crunch."

"Yeah, crunch," Nora said.

Silence hovered between them, snow beginning to coat their shoulders.

Brian broke the quiet before it became deafening. "What do you say we get the kids inside where it's warm, then we can figure out what to do . . . about this." He spread his hands before the damage to her car. The truck appeared fine, just old and apparently indestructible.

Nora had other ideas about what she wanted to do, high on the list was wringing this guy's neck. Her car! But she knew Brian was right, get the kids out of the cold, deal with things then. Mother mode before lawyer, she told herself.

She could hear her mother's words ring inside her mind, telling her that Brian is very practical and wise, and he had an easy, calming nature to his six-foot frame. No wonder Gerta liked to be around him, he had soothed her during a difficult transition period. Now it was Nora facing one, but she didn't need his bit of calm. She had no need for the services of Brian Duncan.

She gave him one last look. Even after an accident he had an affable way about him, from the gee-whiz smile to the thick brown hair where snowflakes were making him gray. Then she couldn't resist taking one last look at the damage to her car, wondering if it was repairable. She wondered if the same applied to her.

"What's that they say?" Brian was asking.

Nora realized Brian was still talking to her. "I'm sorry, I must have zoned out. What did you say?"

"They say most car accidents occur when you're almost home."

Words failed Nora. What he'd said, she knew it was just another of those homespun adages courtesy of the quaint village of Linden Corners, yet the words rang deep inside her. She craned her neck to look over at her childhood home, so close she could almost touch it.

Yup, almost home. And it was no accident she was here.